# Osteen Three

## Deanna F Miller

PublishAmerica
Baltimore

Hardcover 978-1-4626-0408-1
Softcover 978-1-4626-0409-8
PUBLISHED BY PUBLISHAMERICA, LLLP
www.publishamerica.com
Baltimore

Printed in the United States of America

*To my mom, who gave me the courage to write.*

*To Sandy, because she said she would read it.*

*To my sisters, without them, I would have nothing to write.*

*To Keith, for loving me.*

*And to my darling daughter, Aryanna, who loves books as much as her mommy does.*

# *One*

"You know we are going to have to help her, right?" Rebecca asked Sheridan.

"Yeah, I know, I just don't know when, Lilly isn't really ready for this, she just got here, Beck. We can't force her into this right now."

"I know Sher, but Joan needs help, the help only the three of us can do, you know that. And Lilly has been back for six weeks now. How much more healing time does she need? It took me 2 weeks to heal from the garbage Doug dished out. Let's go, let's get over it and move on." Beck dropped into the over stuffed chair in Sheridan's home library. She had come over an hour earlier than planned, just to talk about her older sister. Rebecca was the youngest of the three. She was turning 38 October 31st and felt like she was turning 18 again. She couldn't understand why anyone would need this long to get over a cheating liar, and said as much.

"She needs to get laid, correctly, she needs to put that prick behind her and stop sobbing over him, I mean really, what did he ever do for her?" Beck asked Sher.

"You know, not everyone is, for lack of a better word, as heartless as you, and you know I don't mean that in a bad way. You just have this gift to cut people off right away, not everyone can do that Beck, give her time. And in Lilly's defense, she loved that 'prick" Sher stole a look at Beck and understood her frustration. Lilly was taking this hard, too hard. Steve was a jerk. Always had been. Even before they got married. Beck and Sher never saw what drew Lilly to him. But something did, and they married and had three daughters. Well, the best part of Steve was their daughters.

"I don't cut people out without good cause, Sher. And why shouldn't I? You gonna lie to me? No. Get out of my life, I don't need that. You gonna cheat on me? Again no. Get out. You gonna hit me? Abuse my emotions? No and no. I'm not heartless, I love, I feel, I want

*and* I cry, just the same as you and Lilly. But as Gran always said "screw me once shame on you, screw me twice, shame on me. Words to live by, my sister."

With a laugh and sigh, Sheridan hugged her little sister and went to open the door for her older sister.

"How did you know I was here, I didn't even knock. I made no sound. How do you do that?" Lilly asked.

"My gift." As she took Lilly's purse she handed her a drink, "And a margarita is your gift"

They went to the library again and settled in, the view from here was the best. With the french doors open, the marsh breeze swept all around them. The salt air was one of the things they all loved, the house was the first love they all felt. It was their home, where they grew up, where their mother and grandmother grew up. It's where they shared their secrets and their tragedies.

As they sat in silence for several minutes, each sister in her own thoughts, the breeze picked up and enveloped them.

"I want to be normal again" Lilly said. "I want to be happy and feel loved. I'm tired of feeling like I've failed my kids and myself." She sipped her drink as she waited for her sisters to give her advice she new she wouldn't really use. But tonight, she wants to feel like she was as strong as the two of them are, so she put herself out there. For her sisters to take apart and put back together. And tonight, she'd listen to them.

Sher and Beck looked at each other over their drinks. Very seldom did Lilly let them have their say with her personal life. So they knew with this open question, this question of help, that she must be at bottom. Before either of them spoke, they thought. Knowing their sister as they did, they would have to choose each word with care. One wrong move, and Lilly would close to them, and it would be the end of the evening for them all.

'Lilly, you are not a failure, and I'm sorry he has made you feel like that. You have great accomplishments in your life, don't let him do this to you." Beck hated to see either of her sisters in pain. Especially from the hands of a piece of trash like Steve.

"She's right," Sher said. "You didn't cause the end of your marriage, nor did you cause the pain in your children. You are the one that is here, with the girls, trying to repair the damage Steve did. And I'd say you're doing a great job. The girls were here the other day, and they were as crazy as ever. The laughter they put out filled this house to the brim. That my friend is very far from failure. To hear your children laugh, is a gift from the Gods."

Lilly sighed, long and deep. The girls haven't laughed in such a long time. Always walking around her so quietly, afraid they might break her. She longed to hear their laughter again.

"I wish they'd laugh with me." Lilly said. The pain in her voice was thick. "They think they can't laugh because I hurt. I miss them. We live in the same house. I see them every day and I miss them. I need to reconnect with them. I just don't know what to say right now. I don't want to bring anything up that will hurt them, Gods they have been hurt enough." With her words she didn't know what she had said. Her sisters smiled at her. "Gods" was her way of coming back to them. "Gods" was her small, and unknown to her, way of embracing her gifts. Her magic. And with a small shine in her eyes, the magic took hold of her again. Even though she had cast it aside for her husband, her magic never left her. And with that one word, her sisters knew it would be ok. She would be ok again. So the mood of the library switched. Instead of Sher and Beck telling her what to do, they listened as she told her self what she needed to do. And the salty breeze grew sweeter.

"Give the girls some credit, Lilly. They know how much hurt you hold. And they also know everything he has done. I think you should clear the air. Talk honest with them. They have things to say too. They need to talk to you. It will cleanse you all. "

"You're right Sher, it's the new start we need. That's our first step. And I can't go forward until we put this to rest. I knew you two were good for something." And the laughter between the three sounded like music to the few on the beach who were lucky enough to hear it.

As the minutes ticked by, and the hours ran into each other, the three sisters got back to ease. They knew each other so well, the way their minds worked, what they were thinking when a look came to their face. And here on the rock patio, with the moon shining across the water, they simply were.

As Beck looked at her sisters, she had a strange feeling of dread. She couldn't pin point it, but knew something was coming. Something or someone was coming and one of her sisters would be devastated by it. She told them what she felt.

There was no reason not to. What ever was about to happen, all three would deal with it.

At the end of the night, when Beck and Lilly kissed and hugged Sher good night, they walked to Lilly's car. Beck stood with the door opened and looked across the yard to the marsh, the full moon laid a thin white line across it. "It's beautiful, isn't it?" Beck asked Lilly. "Makes you think all is right with the world when you stop and see beauty like that. "

"All will be right soon enough Beck, with all our worlds. But I had the same feeling you did tonight, that feeling of dread. I don't know what it is, but something's coming. Maybe just a storm" Beck knew as well as Lilly, no storm could make the two of them feel that feeling. And Beck wondered if Sher had it to. If not, then maybe what's coming is for her.

"Do you think Sher felt it too?" Beck asked Lilly

"I don't know, I'll ask her later, right now I just want to go home and see my girls,"

"Yeah, me too." Beck answered softly.

When Lilly dropped Beck off they hugged and said good night, before Lilly drove off Beck leaned down through the window.

"Its going to be ok, maybe not tomorrow or the next day, but it will one day be ok again." She smiled at her sister, warm and loving.

"I know it will, I'm not as strong as you and Sher, No Beck, I'm not, but that's ok. Ill get there, in my own time, my own way. Don't push and no spells. I mean it

Beck, Let me do this, or I'll never get up and do anything on my own. Love you, get off my car and let me go home." Beck stood back, and she drove off.

"You will be ok, Lilly, and I will use magic." Beck said to her self.

# *Two*

The next morning, Beck got up early and sat on her own deck and listened as her world woke. The birds and bugs of summer, then her girls came. Or the two that still lived at home. Reese came out first with a glass of juice and toast, she was the kind of girl that slept hard, and you didn't talk to her until she talked first. Her red gold hair was in a braid that fell past her butt. Her beautiful almond shaped hazel eyes were heavy with sleep. Beck watched as the morning took hold of her. Her gradual waking.

"How is Aunt Lil?" Reese asked.

"Better, "Beck answered.

"We all went out for pizza last night, after you went to Aunt Sher's. Steph told us about the divorce. Well, what is leading to the divorce? Uncle Steve's a pig, we all agree." Reese said with out much emotion. That's one of the best things about her daughter. Reese never minced words. She calls a spade a spade. If she thought it, she said it. Regardless. All her girls were like that. But Reese had a way about it. She was smooth with the truth. Never sugar coated. But soft, as she told you what she thought. You never had to question what she was thinking.

"Yeah I agree with you. Are the girls ok with what's going on?" Beck asked.

"I guess so. Steph and Sarah talked about it, but Savannah was quiet. She didn't say much. I don't think she knew everything that he was doing, well up until last night." Reese finished her breakfast and headed inside to get ready for her day. She and Rowan where headed to Becks oldest daughters new apartment to help paint.

"What time are you two leaving?" Beck asked Rowan when it was her turn to join her mom for breakfast.

"I don't know, an hour maybe." Rowan had more of her mother's features than all of her girls. Her hair was thick and long, with more of a dark amber color with light highlights. Her eyes where hazel as well, all four of them had the same color eyes. Some times Beck was mistaken for one of their sisters instead of their mother. This was not a problem for Beck.

"When I get done with inventory at the store, want me to come and help? Or is this a private sister thing?"

"No come, please, the more people the faster we get it done." Rowan said.

"Rory said you all talked about Aunt Lil. And that Savannah was quiet."

"Yeah, she knew I think, what Steve did. And I refuse to call him Uncle any more. She knew what he was doing. But it was confirmed more or less last night. We talked about all of you three really." With that, Rowan laughed. "We fixed all of your lives. And swore we won't be like our mothers. Instead, we will be like our

Aunts." With that Rowan got up, kissed her mother and left.

"You, my dear child, are just like me I'm sorry to tell you. So, get over yourself."

She loved her girls. All three of them were great kids. They gave her trouble. Buy the Gods they did. But she wouldn't have it any other way. That's the way kids grow, and learn. And to Beck, she wanted her girls to always grow and learn. Like her mother let her do. Her childhood was a happy one. Her father was a Navy man. Her mother stayed home with them. They could always count on her. Dad was gone most of the time, 9 months of the year. Somehow their mom made it work.

Money was always tight. But she never went without. Their vegetables were grown in the back garden and they all helped. It was a Saturday morning ritual. They all helped and they all got their hands dirty. Both her mother and grandmother taught them to garden and they all seemed to have a green thumb. She remembers finding them in the garden every morning. She could hear her gran laughing and her mother telling stories of what mischief her daughters were into. She never got 'grounded". She was never punished in the same way her friends were. The look of disappointment on her mothers face was enough. Well, most of the time. But sometimes she just had to be free. And do what she needed and wanted to do. That seemed to be the trait she never got over. She still did what she wanted when she wanted. For Beck that was both a blessing and a curse. She cleared the table and put the dishes in the sink and left them to wait for later. She took herself to her room and dressed for the day. She had closed the store today so she could do the inventory that she tried to do once a year. To her, she knew what she had and what she needed. Without writing it down all the time. But the accountant said he needed to know everything in the store now so he could renew the insurance. So she would suffer through counting. Maybe with a little luck her sisters would come to help.

She heard the girls call out their goodbyes to her, the front door slam, and Rowan's car pull from the drive. She showered, dressed, and headed for the front door when a smell stopped her in her tracks. Her home was perfumed with smells of Ambrosia, but this was not Ambrosia. It was an earthy smell she couldn't put her finger on. A damp musky smell, almost of rot. She walked through the hall and into her own library where the smell was heavy in the air.

"Whose here?" she asked out loud. She stood in the middle of the room with the silence echoing around her. All she could hear was the sound of her heart beating in her ears.

"I know you're here, what do you want?" Again she asked, and again she got no answer. As the minutes ticked by, the smell faded until it was gone. And although the smell had disappeared, Beck couldn't help but feel that there was something still in her home.

Beck unlocked the front door to the store and quickly went in, she left the blinds pulled and the closed sign in the window, but didn't lock the door. If someone still came in, she figured they really needed her help and she wouldn't refuse. Her store was set on the main "tourist" road at the end. She had bought the building so that she could paint it or redecorate it the way she had always dreamed a store she owned would look. Black on the outside with jasmine and moon flowers growing up the front walls to the second story balcony. She had the windows reframed with old bricks from one of the side streets that was torn up and pavement poured. A shame she thought. A shame most of the towns people thought. But the old brick gave her store front just the look she wanted. Old. She had an arbor at the front entrance with red Mandeville growing around it. Her sign which read "Sisters Three" was made to look aged as well. She had been here for 12 years now, but the sign made it look as if it had been her for hundreds of years. And as far as she was concerned, it was. Her mother, grandmother and great grandmother never owned a store on St George Street. That generation sold their secrets from their back porch. The same goods as Beck was selling now. A few items she sold went to teenage girls looking for magic love spells, or tourists buying novelty items. But she had regulars, who understood her magic, and their own. Most of the customers were from here and took Beck at her word.

Nowhere in her life was she as orderly as she was inside the store. She knew where everything was, and when something was missing. Within seconds of walking in the door she could tell if something was out of place. And it always was. She had her own haunts inside the store. That's why she was able to get the price she wanted when she bought. No one else wanted it. But to her, it was a bonus to buy the shop complete with ghost. And her ghost was mischievous, not threatening. It was a game just the two of them played. She had named her ghost Alice. See, after she had bought the building, she went to the historical society and researched it. She had found out that the site of her store had once been a two room home where a single mother and her daughter had lived. The mother had come upon hard times and had but one way to make a living, and feed her young daughter. However, one night when a regular came to call, a quarrel about price erupted. He beat her unconscious and her house was lit afire. He did not know that her daughter was hiding in the crawl space, under the house. She died at the age of 5. Alice, however, never left the site of her home. Even when a new house went up. She stayed. And she was a typical 5 year old. She bumped into Becks customers, she pulled on their dresses or sleeves for attention. Sometimes when Beck was alone in the store, she could hear Alice playing in the front of the store. Beck would just listen to her laughs and giggles and leave her to what ever she was up to. On occasion things got broke. But all Beck ever said to Alice was "please be careful". She never once yelled or complained. Beck figured Alice had all the rights the Gods could give her to play and laugh and break things. Her life on earth had been cut short due to an argument over money. Beck would not complain to her about breaking something that cost money to replace. And nothing in the store was worth the loss of Alice's laughter in the stillness of the night.

This morning a statue of Isis was missing. It wasn't broken or lost. Just missing. And Beck knew that through out the day she would find it, talk with Alice and put it back. The game of hide and seek was an easy one to play. And she knew all too well that Alice deserved to play something fun. In death that was not in life.

"Ok Alice, so it's Isis again is it?" Beck asked, with no answer. "Well alright, that seems to be the favorite thing to move, let's see how well you've hidden it today". As Beck moved through the store. She could tell that Alice was close to her. She could smell the fire that still clung to her and "feel" the change in the air. She made her way to the back of the store and into the "kitchen" area. She made some coffee and sat with her inventory books. She knew how to work a computer, but still liked the feel of the old book that her Great Gran had started. Before she opened it, she smoothed her hand across the cover. This was one of the oldest things she owned. Her mother had handed it to her the day she opened her store. She had memories of this book. She could see her Gran and great grandmother at the kitchen table, filling in things the neighbors had purchased or traded. Bags of flour or eggs. Sometimes bars of soap, and even bouquets of flowers. Her great grandmother, Ilthia, turned nothing down. She would always accept whatever payment could be made. She never gave anything for free. She would tell her girls that it made the patrons feel better about themselves if they made a payment and that there was nothing more important than how you felt about yourself. She could see Ilthia as if she were still here. She remembers the nights the neighbors would come for her potions, for sickness or love. The desperation of the women's faces to make their men stay home, or fall back in love with them. And always late night visits. Ilthia had told us it wasn't always late night. There was a time when her goods were respectable. There was a time when doctors would come to her. When new mothers with babies with colic would ask for her help. But as time went by, she was considered a crazy old woman. It never seemed to bother her, she would always laugh and say it was true. But even with the talk of her being crazy and her potions being for the

simple minded, they still knocked on her door. The mayor with a sick child, the teacher with a wandering husband. They all came, but they came under the cover of darkness and the forgiveness of church on Sunday.

Ilthia didn't care, she sold to those who needed, and never refused to help. Well, that's not completely true. Beck could remember one night, when she was about 6. She and her sisters were sitting on the stairs listening to her mother, grandmother and Ilthia trying to tell one of the teachers why they couldn't do what she was asking for…

In the middle of the night, while the house was sleeping, just before midnight, Beck woke with a start. She sat upright in bed and listened. She didn't know if she was dreaming or if she heard something, a cry of help maybe. A few minutes later both Sher and Lilly had come into her room.

"Something's coming," Sher said.

Lilly was quiet, just listening to the air around them.

The minutes ticked by. All three girls sat watching out the window for something. They didn't know what, but they knew something was coming.

"Mom's up," Lilly said in a whisper. "And so is gran and Nona."

As the house came slowly alive around her, the outside did as well. The three girls sat at the window. Looking for the mysterious reason they all were awake. And then they heard it. A low groan coming off the marsh. A sound that terrified all three girls.

"What is it?" Lilly asked.

"It's a woman." Sher had said.

"It can't be, not making that noise." But before Lilly could say more, they saw the lights of a boat come across the marsh. And the sounds of a woman crying for help. She had called out to her Gran. And her gran had replied. The girls could tell at once who it was, and what it was she carried.

"Clare, we can't do that." Her mother, Athena, said.

"But I have seen you do all sorts of things, please, please do this for me!" As they listened to Clare or Mrs. Smith as they knew her from school, Beck remembers the anguish in her voice.

"But Clare, we have never done this for anyone, and we just can't. What would come back, it's not natural. I'm sorry, we can help with your grief, and we can help you to sleep, but we just can't help you with your daughter." Athena looked to her mother and grandmother for support.

Which she had, neither women would attempt what it was Clare wanted.

Clare covered her face with trembling hands and sobbed into them. The three women at the table were silent while Clare let some of her grief out.

"Why her? She was my world, she was my baby. It's not fair, it's just so not fair." Clare had lost her daughter. She had drowned in the swamp the night before. And Clare had lost her mind. She had only one chance for a child. And now that was taken from her.

"I can't, I just can't do this. I don't want to live without her. Please, I know you have something that can bring her back to me."

"Child" My gran said "we will not be able to help you with this, as Athena has told you. What would come back would not be your beautiful daughter, but something evil and ugly. We will not do that to you, or most of all, to her. Let her beauty sleep with the Gods who have called her home to them"

This enraged Clare. She jumped up from her chair and knocked it over.

"Her home is with me!" the pain etched on her face, in her voice. "I want her here with me! I'm her mother, I'm the one who loves her and needs her"

Clare left the house carrying her daughter's body. And the next day she was buried. A week later so was Clare.

When Beck finished inventory, after every last item in the store was carefully written in her book, 4 hours had passed. She sat at her desk and stretched.

"That's enough" She said to Alice. Then it dawned on her, she had not come across the Isis statue. She looked at her watch and thought she had a few minutes to hunt for it before going to Rory's.

"Ok Alice, give me a hint" She made her way through the second story rooms of the store.

# *Three*

When Lillianna finally got herself out of bed, she found the girls had cleaned the house for her. She found the note the girls had left for her. "Gone to Rory's" So she was alone in the house. The large two story was one of the older homes in the Abbott tract, built in the late 18oo's. It had once been in her family and she had some memories of the house. Mostly in the kitchen. She had the option to buy, but for now she was happy to rent something big enough for them all that was familiar enough to be comfortable. She made herself coffee and looked out the kitchen window to the small yard. The neighbors had all built privacy fences, which in turn made her yard private as well. She took her coffee to the small back porch, set it on an end table and walked to the side yard to grab the paper. She returned to the porch and settled herself in one of the wicker chairs. As she read through the "mullet wrapper" her mind drifted to the problem at hand. She laid the paper down, closed her eyes, and let her mind wander to the night she had told Steve she wanted a divorce.

"I can't believe you are going to rip our family apart like this Lil." Steve had said to her.

"I'm going to rip the family apart? Me? How do you figure this is MY fault? I'm not the one sleeping around, and don't try to deny it, I know you are, and I know you have been for years."

She could hear him thinking of a way out of this, she knew he was a master at lies. He had been lying to her from the beginning. What was that 22 years now?

"Where are my daughters?' He asked her in a strangely calm voice.

"They are with friends, at the movies I think."

What did they have to do with this? Lil thought! Why was he so calm? I just told him I was leaving him with the girls, going home.

"If you think I'm going to let you take my girls, you're crazy. I don't care where you go, but not with my kids."

"Your kids? They are more mine than yours, Steve. You don't even have time to talk to them when you show up. You aren't here when they need help with home work, or boys, or any of their games. Besides, they want to go with me."

"That's because you are filling their heads with lies about me. You told them that I am cheating on you! So now they will hate me, right? That's what you've done isn't it!" He stood up and grabbed the table with both hands and slung it across the room. Before, Lil would cower. She would try and console him when his anger got out of control. This would be the time that she usually apologized to him and would try all she could to take back what she had always accused him of. On the few times that she had tried to stand her ground, he had slapped her.

"That won't work any more, Steve. I don't care if you break the house apart. I don't care if you slap me again, I'm leaving and the girls are coming with me. There's nothing you can do about it". With that Lil stood up and started out of the kitchen. She was shaking inside, her stomach was rolling with nerves. She always knew he could hurt her. But she had always backed down before. This time, she wasn't going to.

"You think you can just tell me you are leaving with my kids and walk away from me?' It took him three steps to catch her. He grabbed her by the arm and turned her to face him.

"Let me go, you're hurting me"

"Ill let you go when I have told you what we are going to do about this. I'm not letting you take my kids and make me out to be a fool to all of our friends."

"So that's it, you don't want our friends to know what a fuck you are. You aren't concerned at all for the girls and me, it's your reputation that you care most about. You are such a jerk."

And with that, he slapped her. Harder then usual. Lil hit the floor and clutched her face. The burn from the slap making her eyes water. She knew that an outline of his hand was on her cheek. She turned to look at him, and slowly stood up.

"You're a man, aren't you?" And just as she stood straight up, het slapped her again. This time with more force. Lil knew she should stay down. She could see in his eyes the danger she was now in. She had been fooling herself to believe he wouldn't go this far. That he'd

never really hurt her. He was about to. And she had no way to get out of it. Stay down is what her mind kept saying to her. But somewhere deep inside, her pride started to awaken. In the few seconds it took her to hit the floor and get back up, all she could think of, what if this was my daughter? What if my daughter could see this? Would she be proud of a mother who would stay down? And with that, she stood back up.

"You can beat me all you want Steve, I'm still leaving you and the girls are still coming with me."

"Call them home Lil, now"

"No" was all she said. Once again she tried to make it out of the kitchen and once again he hit her, and with each hit, she stood back up, until she had reached the front door. Her face was bloodied, and her head throbbing with pain. When she tried to open the door, with no more strength then a kitten, he blocked her.

She rested her head against the door and began to cry. She could hear Steve behind her, his breathing was strong and harsh. He leaned his body against hers and whispered in her ear,

"You will never leave this house, Lil. Do you hear me? Never. At least not alive." He began to run his fingers through her hair. And then down her arm. She knew what he wanted. What he was planning. She could feel his hardness on her back. He turned her around and the self satisfied look in his eyes turned her stomach. He put both hands on her face and tried to kiss her. She slowly reached to side table and slipped the strap of her purse around her wrist. As he relaxed and kissed her stronger, she brought her knee up with all the might that she had. A howl of pain ripped through his mouth as he backed up and grabbed for his crotch. She flung the door open and ran for her SUV. She reached for her keys and hit the button to unlock the doors. She made it inside and locked the doors just as Steve grabbed the handle to open them. A second too late she thought. He was a mere second too late. He screamed at her to open the door. He told her she'd never get away from him. He ranted and raved at her while she took a minute to gain her strength back. She slipped her hand inside her purse and pulled out a digital recorder. When he saw what she had in her hands, he stopped. It took a minute for him to realize what it was she was

showing him. And then he knew. She had taped the entire thing. The arguing, the beating he had given her. The threat on her life if she left him. He backed up from the SUV. She started the engine and backed up. All the time never taking her eyes off him. As she drove around the block she dialed Stephanie, her oldest daughter. She told her to meet her outside the movies, alone.

"MOM!! What happened" Steph said when she got into the SUV with her mom. "Oh My God! Did dad do this to you?" Lil didn't know what to say, she had nowhere to turn but to her daughter. And she hated herself for doing this. But the friends that she had were really Steve's and she knew she couldn't go to any of them.

"Yes, I told him tonight I was taking you girls back home and that I wanted a divorce." Lil began to cry again. Only this time it wasn't for the pain. It was for what she was about to ask of her daughter.

"I need help, Steph. I think I need to go to the ER. I think he broke my jaw and I can't focus on anything. I don't know what to do with your sisters. You all can NOT go home tonight, but I don't want you out of my sight."

"I'll take them to Connie's or Irene's or something."

"No honey, no one that your father knows. I don't want him to get to them somehow."

"Ok" Steph thought for a minute. "How about Lisa's?"

"Ok, that will work, take them there and then meet me back here. How long will it take you to get there?'

"I can be back in like, 20 minutes."

With that she watched Steph drive off with her other two daughters. After they were out of sight, she dialed 911.

She opened her eyes again and found she had been crying. The thoughts of what he could do to her scared the hell out of her. But she hadn't heard from him since that night. Everyday that went by made her more nervous at what he may be planning. She had taken some things from the house before he had come home that night. Mostly the girl's things. She really didn't care if she got more or not. They were doing fine with what they had. She had some money stashed away from her inheritance. They weren't rich, she was going to have to look for work soon. But at least she could take it easy for a little while and try to sort her life out. She knew the girls had questions for her. Thankfully they hadn't asked anything yet. In truth, she had no answers, yet. She got up and went inside to dress for the day. She would meet the girls at Rory's and then go shopping. Three girls really could clean out a refrigerator as well as boys. At least hers could. On her way up the stairs to her room, she stopped in the front parlor, her guitar was leaning against the side wall where she had left it since she had left Steve. She hadn't touched it since then. She didn't feel the music inside her now. Like it had died the night she left him.

"It's not dead." She said to herself. "It's just resting, like me." She pulled the guitar to her and laid it on her lap. She carefully strummed it and tuned it. Before she knew it, she was playing a melody she had written for Savannah when she was born. The melody moved her in a way nothing else could. She closed her eyes and strummed. Music always lifted her and made her feel whole again. It was like the pieces of her life were joined in the music. The more she played, the more it came together. Her mind played back times with her girls. The birth of Stephanie, Sarah's first day of school and the way Savannah laughed. When she was done, she laid it down.

"Thank you" she whispered and went up the stairs before she heard the whispered reply "You're welcome"

A few hours later she and the girls were on their way to Wal-Mart. Food was their main goal. Though she knew they would never get out of there for less then two hundred dollars.

At dinner, when she was off guard, Sarah asked the question she knew was coming.

"So, what's up with dad?" The conversation came to a stop. Lilly just looked at her plate trying to figure out what she would tell them,

"Sarah, come on, leave mom alone."

"No, its ok, Steph, I know you girls want to know what's going on, and thanks you for giving me some time before you asked." Lilly stopped her for a minute. Trying to get herself together and decided she was going to answer their questions truthfully. Not because she wanted them to be mad at their dad. But because she had always told them the truth before, and she saw no reason to stop now. If they asked, she was going to tell. They deserved that.

"Well, we are getting divorced, honey."

"Yeah we know that, but what happened the night we drove here. Steph won't tell us, and we know something bad happened. Mom there's not enough make up to cover the bruises on your face. He hit you didn't he?" Sarah asked, but she already knew the answer. She just needed to hear it from her mom.

"Yes, he hit me. I told your dad I was taking you three with me and I wanted a divorce. He got very mad, and hit me."

"Has he hit you before?" Her sweet innocent Savannah asked.

"Yes honey." Was all she could bring herself to say. Savannah thought her dad was great. That he hung the moon. To find out that he was really a monster, she just didn't want to be the one to tell her that.

They all sat in silence for several minutes. The girls absorbed what Lilly was telling them. She could see on all their faces the wheels spinning in their minds. And she waited.

"How long? I mean how long has he been hitting you?" Sarah asked.

Gods she hated this. She hated Steve for putting her here.

"It started about 6 months after we got married." Lilly told them in almost a whisper.

"MOM!" the three said in unison. "Why would you stay? Why didn't you make him stop?" Steph finished. Lilly put her hands to her face and breathed deep.

"I don't know what to tell you girls. I stayed for you, I stayed for me. I stayed because it was my life. I didn't think that I could make it on my own, especially with three daughters." When she uncovered her face, she saw the looks on their faces and quickly said

"I'm NOT blaming my stupidity on you three. Do not look like that. I don't blame anything on you girls. This is something that I did. Not you." She looked at each of her daughters until they believed her and they relaxed.

"Now,' Lilly said, 'That's it. I made a mistake by staying as long as I did. But I'm fixing it now. I need to build a life for us here. You all can call him and see him anytime you want. I won't keep you from him. I would appreciate you letting me know if he plans on coming here to see you and you all meeting him somewhere other then here. I myself don't want to see him again. Now, let's finish dinner and get some sleep. School tomorrow."

# *Four*

"I talked to the girls last night" Lilly said to her sisters.

"And how did that go?" Sher asked.

"As well as can be expected. Sarah loves her dad, I popped that bubble."

"No Lilly, HE popped that bubble. You didn't beat the crap out of yourself." Beck told her.

"Yeah, I know, but somehow this feels like my fault." She leaned back in her chair and closed her eyes. "I haven't heard a damn thing from him either. That is scaring the hell out of me. I should have heard from him or a lawyer."

"Do you have a lawyer yet?" Sher asked

"No, I haven't gotten that far yet. I don't know if I want anything from the house or not. Id like to get some of the girls things, But I don't want to call and ask him. I was wondering if the girls were gonna call him or not. Steph said something last night about calling him today and getting him to send her computer and stuff to her. But I don't know if he will or not. The night I left, he really didn't care that we were leaving, just that his friends would find out. You know?"

"Well, if you want me to, I know a few lawyers that will help you out at hardly any cost. Not free just cheap."

Lilly got up and poured another drink for each of them. Again they were at Sher's. A night with just the three of them. They had met like this once a week since Lilly came back.

"That would be good, have them call my cell."

She came back to her sisters and handed them the drinks.

"You know, I've never been alone before. I know I'm not really alone, I have the girls. But I mean, I went from mom and dad's to Steve. I have never done it on my own before. I have always been the one to pay the bills and stuff. But never the one to earn it. We never counted on the money I made to get us through. And that reminds me, I need a job. I was thinking about teaching again. Maybe a music class or maybe private lessons."

"I'm glad you're back." Beck said. "I know you'll be ok, I know what you feel like right now. Like you have failed. But things will get better. You have us and all the girls to count on. You won't be alone unless you want to be. Again, I'm glad you're back." Beck and Lilly stared at each other.

"OK, that's enough about him. He consumed me last night, I don't want to dwell on him any more tonight. Let's just talk about random crap. Halloween, you still having a party Beck?"

"Hell yes, costume party every year. This year's theme is pirates. That gives us girls a bit of sexy and the men can unleash their alter egos. And it gives you about 3 weeks to get ready." Beck said with a smile.

"Well, I'm sure I can pull something together. As for my girls, no sexy yet."

They talked about nothing for the next couple of hours. Just let themselves get used to each other again. They made plans to go to the costume stores together and what each of them should bring to the party. They talked about the schools the girls were attending and Sher and Beck clued her into the teachers. Which ones were great and the ones not so much.

Lilly told them she was worried about Sarah the most. She seemed to be very quiet, more so then normal.

Beck and Sher looked at each other, "What?" Lilly asked.

"Nothing really" Sher said.

"NO, I know that look between the two of you, what's up?"

"Well, there's something we need to talk to you about and we've kinda been waiting 'til the time was right and you got all settled in."

"Well, I'm in so what gives?"

"We need your help." She said, looking straight into Lilly eyes. And Lilly knew what kind of help they were talking about.

# *Five*

Sher knew this was not going to be easy for Lilly. She had long ago put her powers away for her soon to be ex husband, Steve. He thought her stupid and silly. And she had always had trouble with the things she could do. Even before Steve. He just added shame to it. Now she and Beck were about to ask her to bring it out again, like it was a favorite toy or something. But they needed help from her. There was no way she and Beck could do this without Lilly. This was going to be a very long night, but it had to be done.

"Listen to us before you say no, Lilly. Just stop for a minute and listen, please." Sher said.

"We know that you haven't practiced in what, 18 years or more? And we know why. But we can't do this with out you. A friend of ours is in real trouble and we want to help. And we have tried everything that we can think of. But it's going to take all three of us to do this." Beck said to Lilly.

"Or else we wouldn't ask." Sher added. Lilly had turned her head away from her sisters. Her eyes closed and old memories coming back was not what she wanted tonight. She just wanted to be free of stress for a while. In her mind she thought, must be too much to ask.

"I, we, know how you feel about this Lilly, but hear us out and think about it first." Stressed Beck. When she saw Lilly turn her head she knew Lilly was tuning them out.

"All right, give it your best shot." Was all Lilly could say. She turned to look at her sisters. And waited for them to tell the story.

"Joan works at the store part time for me," Beck started. "She bought a house on Saragossa Street, close to the cemetery and she is having a hell of a time with, well, you know... spooks."

Lilly was quiet for a minute, she rubbed her hands across her face and got up to walk to the patio. Beck and Sher followed her.

"You know, I haven't even thought about stuff like this in years. You two know better than anyone how I feel about this stuff. I don't even know if I can still help, that is if I wanted to." Lilly was talking to her sisters, but looking out into the marsh. She could hear the cicadas and crickets. A harmony of the south. In a few weeks there would be no sounds like this. Winter would be here by then. And the marsh would be quieter. Not silent, but quieter. She breathed in the salt air and watched the cranes fly. Lilly turned to her sisters and said "OK, I'll help." Sher and Beck went to hug her, but Lilly put her arm up. "Wait, before you get all happy and set this up for tomorrow, you have to give me a bit of time. I need to re-connect to this gift I have."

"That's fine, that's understandable. We get it, how much time are you talking about?" Beck asked.

"A week? Can I have a week to brush up on this? "

Both Sher and Beck agreed.

"Ok, tell me what's going on in the house? Guess I should have asked that first." She laughed.

"She's got a ghost, duh, but he's not a good one. He seems to have started out hiding stuff of hers, keys, and shoes. Stuff like that. Then it went to bigger things, closing doors, opening all the cabinets. Now he's all the way to slamming doors in her face. Pulling covers off her in the middle of the night. Screaming her name any time of day. The cats are both gone. And she has been sleeping at her friends for the past week." Beck explained.

"She now knows why the house was so cheap." Sher said

"Aren't they supposed to tell you all these things about the house *before* you buy it?" Lilly asked.

"I thought so, that's what I heard. But this was a 'By owner' so it could be different." Beck said. "The point is, Joan wants to keep the house. We just have to figure a way to get him out."

"Have you two already gone over there?" Lilly asked them.

"Yeah, a few times. We tried a few things, but Joan said we really only irritated it. That's why we need you as well. The three of us."

"And why do you keep saying 'he'?"

"I saw him" Sher said. "I saw a man at the foot of her bed. We tried to chant him out. We tried the candles and salts. But he wouldn't leave her room."

"I heard him once" Beck said. "A very firm 'NO' in my ear. And tell you what, it freaked me out a little bit."

"It freaked you out?" Lilly asked teasingly. "I didn't think anything freaked the 'I'm all great and wise in the magical area'." With that they laughed.

"I'm just telling you, do what you need to get ready, cuz I think we have a fight on our hands." Beck said to Lilly

"I suppose you two have a plan already?" Lilly asked them

"We have some thoughts, but we were waiting for you." Sher said to her.

Sher sat back and watched her sisters. She loved nights like this when they were together. Talking about the past, making plans for the future. Lilly had some hard times ahead of her, but Sher knew she'd be ok. Because she was home. Enveloped by her family. The people who loved her.

She remembered the day Lilly moved with Steve to South Carolina. Even though it was within a days drive, it still felt like she was across the sea.

"I'll call as soon as we get there." Lilly told her family.

"Not as soon, we will have things to get done first." Steve told her. Lilly had finished packing the van for the long drive. Steve was getting into the drivers seat.

"Well, we will get settled first and I'll call within a day."

"You won't have time, you'll be unpacking this car, and the movers will be there before us if we don't go now, I mean NOW!" He never let up on her. She was never right about anything. Not even the color of the sky. No one in Lilly's family could understand the attraction she had for him. As far as Sher was concerned Steve was a loser. And he proved it with every word from his mouth. He was conceited, arrogant and a know it all. Most of all he was a phony. You could debate with him, with all the power on your side and prove time and again how wrong he was, but he'd never let up. He'd never let anyone else "win". When it came to Lilly's gift of emotions, he berated her 'til she gave up on what she was once so proud of. She doubted herself at everything she did. She never allowed herself a proud moment.

Sher watched them drive away, with a wave of Lilly's hand from the window, she knew things were about to change. Some for the better, but for Lilly, the change would be for the worse.

# *Six*

"We don't have time to wait for Lilly any more, Joan called last night." Beck told Sher on her cell.

"Hold on a second. I haven't had a cup of coffee yet. Let me call you back."

"No time, Ill grab Lilly on my way to your house. Make us a big pot, we will be there in thirty minutes." Beck hung up on Sher, grabbed her purse. Wrote a note for the girls and left the house. As she drove onto US1, she called Lilly.

"Hello" Lilly answered.

"Sorry to wake you sleeping beauty, but I'm on my way to get you and take you to Sher's, Ill explain when I get there, just get up and get ready." Again she hung up. She pulled up to Lilly's and honked. For the first few minutes they drove in silence.

"This is about Joan, isn't it?"

"Yep. I was on my way to the store when I got her message, that's why I could come get you. Seems our spook is kicking it up a notch. He held her down last night, wouldn't let her up. She was screaming but no one in the house heard her." As they drove to Sher's Beck explained that Joan had friends helping her remodel the house. And that last night they decided to stay the night. One it was late when they finished, and two, they wanted an early start. It was Saturday and they had planned to get a lot done.

They arrived at Sher's within the half hour and found her on the deck with three cups and a pot of coffee.

"Ok, so what happened?" Sher asked.

"She was home with some friends, she said they had been painting the living room and dinning room. They stopped around 11pm for pizza and beers. Joan said there was something all afternoon and night that just wasn't right. But she couldn't figure out what it was. When they finished eating they decided that was enough for the day. She asked them to stay, they did, and crashed in the spare room,

across the hall from her. She said at about midnight she felt something grab her wrist. It jolted her awake. She was screaming for help and couldn't move. She said she could feel someone holding her shoulders. But none of her friends heard her. She swears she screamed for 15 minutes. Finally Sam, who was in the spare room, was going to the bathroom. He said he walked by her room and looked in on her, and she was wrestling with air. That's what he said it looked like. He saw nothing, heard nothing. Once he crossed the threshold into her room, is when he heard her."

"Oh my god. Is she ok?"

"Not really. She packed up some stuff and is staying with Sam. She said she is going to sell the house. I don't blame her. But I did tell her to wait at least a week." Beck looked at

Lilly. Waiting for her to say something. Wanting to ask if and when they might go to the house and see if they can help. Lilly said nothing. Though her mind was racing. She didn't want to go. She was afraid. But she didn't want to leave her sisters to do this alone either.

"Ok, let's make a plan to go tonight." Neither sister said anything to her.

That night Beck picked up Sher and drove to Lilly's. They had brought a few things with them. Candles and salt. Lilly thought that a video and recorder would be helpful. She also had a small amount of black salt.

They drove to Saragossa Street in silence. As they parked, Sher looked at Lilly.

"You ready?"

"Nope, but lets go before I chicken out. And let's NOT touch each other, at least not yet."

They knew that by connecting the three of them together by touch, what they could see, hear and feel became ten times stronger.

Beck walked into the house first, followed by Sher and then Lilly. As soon as all three women were in the house, hell broke loose.

Kitchen cabinets began to open and slam, books flew from shelves. Chairs slid across the room.

"Christ, out out OUT!" Beck yelled. Pushing her sisters out the door.

"What the hell was that?" Lilly asked. Fear had gripped her. She could see it on the faces of her sisters as well. As soon as they walked off the porch, the house was still again. They stood frozen on the side walk. Neighbors peering at them from behind draped windows.

"What was that Beck?" Sher looked at Beck and could see she had no idea it had escalated to this.

"I've never seen that before." Beck said to them. "I don't know what to do here. I mean I've seen things move a little and heard sounds and stuff like that. But I've never seen all that at once!"

Lilly was quiet and Sher started pacing while Beck watched the house.

"Let me go up again and see what happens." Beck said

"I wouldn't go up there right now, Beck, something's in that house and is very pissed off. I could feel so much anger when we went in." Lilly said.

"Let me just go up there, I won't close the door."

"You might not, but whatever's in there might. Here." Sher grabbed a brick and shoved it in her hand. "Put this in the door, so that if it does try to shut, it can't.'

Beck approached the house slowly. She was armed with nothing that could defend her. She opened the door and crossed the threshold again. Both Lilly and Sher held their breath. Waiting for chaos again. Nothing happened.

Beck had laid the brick in the door and continued into the house. It was quiet. She made her way through the downstairs then went up. She went into each room, laying a thick line of salt at each door. Hoping to trap whatever was haunting the house in one of the rooms.

As Lilly and Sher waited, they could hear Beck chanting inside. They came closer to the door to listen and wait for an all clear yell from Beck.

"I don't want to go in there, Sher."

"Neither do I, but I think we should. Besides, I think it used up all its power. There's nothing going on now."

Beck came back to the door, breathless. And a little pale.

"I spread salt at the doors. Nothing happened while I was in there, so come on, let's get this over with."

The three women made their way back into the house, and as soon as Lilly stepped over the threshold, it started again.

"Back out Lilly, just to the other side of the door!" Beck yelled. Lilly scrambled to get to the other side and once she did, it stopped.

"What the hell?" Sher questioned. "I don't get it, does it know Lilly?" Beck and Sher looked at each other then at Lilly.

"No, I don't think so. Sher you go out and Lilly come back in." Beck directed.

As they changed place the house stayed calm.

"It's the three of us, together." Lilly whispered. "How?"

There was no answer. "Well we have got to all be in this house at one time, so we better get ready. Let's just do it." Beck suggested

"No." Lilly stepped out to the porch. "I don't think we need to rush this house like Rambo. I think we need to just hold on and figure something out, have a plan. What do we know about this house? Who lived here before Joan, and before her, etc? When was it built? Let's get together and see if we can figure out who is stuck in this house and why."

They stood in the yard for an hour, deciding who would go to the library and who would go to the historical society. In the end, they decided to go together. Driving back to Lilly's house Beck called and talked with Joan. Telling her to stay with Sam for a few days and that they were going to find some history on the house. Joan said she knew the house was built in 1870 but that was all she knew.

"Joan knows nothing other then the house was built in 1870. She doesn't know who built it or how many families's have lived there or if any one has died in the house."

# Seven

The next morning Beck dropped Sher and Lilly at the historical society.

"I'll go to the library and see what I can find. The best bet will be looking in the city directories first," Sher said to Lilly as they walked up the stairs. The front attendant had them sign in and the director asked if he could help them.

"We are looking for any information on a specific house on Saragossa Street. When it was built and who lived there." Lilly told him.

"Well," He said "the first thing I'd try is the directories, but with out a last name to start, it will be time consuming. But follow me and I'll show you where they are."

The room held two tables and wall to wall shelves. Sher and Lilly dropped their note books and purses on the far table. He pointed out the area in which they would find all the directories

"Now, as you can see, they go back to 1860. But again, with out a name, it will take some time going through it. If you give me the address I can see what I can pull up on the computers." Sher gave him the address and told him anything he might find would be helpful.

Both women picked up several books, sat at the table and began to go thru them. Page after page until they found the address.

For fifteen minutes they sat in silence as they researched the house.

"Look Sher, here's the address," She was excited to have found something so fast. They leaned into the book and read the first of many names.

"Alton Pacetti" They both said out loud.

"This book is from 1905. Look in the ones before and see how long he was there."

They began to search the books before 1905 with fever now. Now that they had a name, and a start.

"Here he is again in 1904 but I can't find him in 1903."

"I can't find the address at all in 1860. I've gone through the book three times now. Guess it was too much to hope for to figure this out in ten minutes."

Lilly sat back in her chair and sighed.

"Well, let's try 1870" She picked up the book and froze. Her eyesight darkened and the room grew cold. Her fingers seemed to be glued to the book in her hands. She could hear voices but could not make out what was being said. She looked around the room to see if any one else was affected. No one was. Not even Sher. She still held onto her book and was reading it with out notice of the change.

Lilly slowly set the book down and turned her eyes to movement by the entrance. In the door way stood a large man. Dressed in black pants and coat. He was staring at her. Only her.

"Sher" Lilly spoke in no more then a whisper. But the tone alerted Sher instantly.

"What do you see Lil."

"There's a man at the door. The room seems to have gone dark and my fingers are freezing. Do you see this at all?"

"I see nothing right now. But I'm cold and the hair on my arms and the back of my neck are sizzling. Who's here?"

"I don't know, he's said nothing to me, just staring at me. Do you think it's the house on Saragossa or this place?"

"Until he says or does something, I don't know."

"Shit, he's coming over here. His mouth is moving, but I don't hear anything. Just a humming noise."

"Relax Lil. See if you can get something from him.'

"What am I supposed to do, Sher, ask him questions, so everyone here can think I'm nuts?"

Sher got up from her chair and started to move to the other side of the table.

Lilly grabbed her arm, "Where are you going! Don't leave me here by myself!"

"I'm just going to the other side of the table, so you can talk to him and it will look like you're talking to me, and you're hurting my arm!"

"Sorry" Lilly let her go.

Sher sat down and pulled her note book to her.

"What's he doing now?"

"He's behind you, still staring at me. I think he's trying to tell me something but I just can't hear anything other then a humming. A kind of bad static radio sound."

Sher's cell phone rang and both women jumped.

She picked up her phone and looked at who was calling.

"It's Beck" Sher answered, "Hello?"

"What's going on? I'm freaking out over here and all I know is something's up with Lilly."

"Beck, we have company, if you know what I mean. I'll call you back"

She snapped her phone shut and looked at Lilly.

"Ask him something, his name, what he wants, something. See if you can get an answer, something you can piece together."

"Oh God, I can't believe I'm doing this. Here goes nothing, or my sanity." Lilly took a deep breath and rubbed her hands together. Before she said anything she looked around the room to see if the other customers were watching her. None were. They were all engrossed in their own books or research.

"Can I help you?' She whispered to the figure. They waited. Lilly glanced at Sher, and shrugged her shoulders.

"Is there something I can help you with?" Again, nothing.

"What is he doing now?" She asked her

"He's just standing there, doesn't even look like he's trying to talk any more." Lilly looked back at Sher.

"What's your name?" they waited.

"He's trying again, I really don't know if he's talking to me or just talking."

Lilly relaxed a bit, once she figured out he wasn't going to hurt them. And still, the other customers knew nothing.

"Wait." Lilly said, "It's something about check the door? Check the floor? Something check? But I can't. I'm sorry" She said looking at the man, "I can't hear you, what is it? What's your name?"

The buzzing grew louder.

"Do you hear that?" Sher asked her.

"Yeah, I think he's getting mad at me. I just can't make it out."

"I can feel him growing Lilly. We need to end this somehow. I'm getting the feeling that he's really getting pissed."

"He is, I can see a change in his facial features. And the buzzing sounds like a freight train now. Something's building.

I think we should leave, Sher." But before they had a chance to stand up, the room imploded in an array of note books and scraps of paper. Chairs fell over and books flew from the shelves. The overhead lights and lamps sizzled with light that was ten times the normal brightness. Then dimmed to normal. A few of the light bulbs in the lamps blew themselves out. Everyone was still. Looking at each other to confirm what they saw was real. For several minutes the library was quiet. Both the director and the assistant ran around asking if everyone was ok. They were trying to straighten up as they went from person to person.

Lilly and Sher just looked at each other.

The urge to run gripped Lilly. Sher could see it.

"Just relax. Lil. Just sit and breathe." All Lilly could think about was getting out of the building and back home where she would be safe.

"I don't think I'm ready for this Sher. What was that? What did he want from us?"

"I don't know. But don't run out of here like a bat out of hell. Just cool it for a minute. Let's think this through."

The books were put back onto the shelves and the papers were neatly stacked on one of the tables. No one spoke louder then a whisper. Still shaken, no one knew what really just happened.

Slowly Sher stood up and began to gather her purse and note books.

"We have a name to start with, let's finish this on the internet for now. There's an ancestry site I'm a member of. Let's go there. If nothing pans, out, well, we will have to come back."

Just as they got to the door, the man who was going to try and help them came up to them.

"I'm sorry I wasn't much help. But I did find this." He gave Sher an old newspaper clipping and turned around.

"What is it?"

"It's an article from the Record, looks like it's from 1901."

As they walked into the bright morning sun, they couldn't shake the chill from the event that took place less than fifteen minutes ago.

# *Eight*

They walked down Artillery to Cordova and down past Flagler College. They were making their way to the house on Saragossa without realizing were they where headed. Their conversation was light. They talked about the differences in the town since they were kids. They enjoyed the cool breeze coming from the bay and the smell of bagels. When they got to the corner of Saragossa and Cordova, Sher's cell phone rang.

"Shit, I forgot to call Beck, crap. Hello?"

"So you keeping me out of this or you gonna tell me what happened?"

"Yeah, where are you?"

"I'm on my way to Lilly's, Why? Were are you?" Beck's temper had calmed some. She realized something bad had happened and that her sisters needed some time to think it over. Try and make some sense of it.

"Come to Joan's. That's were we are headed now, and we'll fill you in on everything that just happened."

"Be there in a minute. See ya."

Sher and Lilly filled Beck in on everything that happened at the historical society. Even the name of the tenant in 1905 and the newspaper article for 1901. The article just talked about A Pacetti doing some remodeling to his home when he returned from a fishing trip in south Florida with his brothers and nephews.

"It's funny that newspapers were printing things like people's vacations. Could you see them doing something like that now?"

Sitting on the porch of Joan's house they talked about random things. What was going on in each other lives, how the girls where doing in school. About Beck's store and Sher's painting classes. They talked about Lilly going back to work and the house she was thinking of buying.

"Well, we have talked our way around the problem at hand. We found out who once owned the house, and that it was built in 1864. It was originally owned by a Pacetti, but I don't think it was Alton. It might have been his father."

"You know, let's go to Lilly's, you got internet yet?" Sher asked.

"Yes we got it last week."

"I can go onto the ancestry site and see if anything comes up when I put his name in."

Back at Lilly's, they made something to eat and then went into the front room that Lilly and the girls were using for an office of sorts. There were still un-packed boxes scattered around.

"Ok, give me a minute and let's see if I can find anything."

While Sher searched the web, Lilly and Beck went out to the front porch and sat on the swing.

"Is this the swing from our family?"

"Yeah, I think so. Looks and feels the same doesn't it?"

"I can't believe they kept it. But I don't think they were here for more than two years. Were they?"

"Not before he took a job in North Carolina, They have asked me several times if I want to buy it back. I don't have an answer for them yet. I need to wait and see what's going to happen after the divorce. I don't know how soon I'll need to get back to work. And what bills I'm going to end up having to pay. Shit like that."

"Hey! You guys, come in here. I think I found him."

Both sisters went to the computer and looked at the screen.

"Looks like Alton Pacetti is a junior. According to the census of 1900, he was born in 1885. He had three sisters as well. His dad is Alton Sr. and this says his birth date is 1860. But by the census of 1905, Alton Sr is gone, the mom is still there, lists her as a widow."

"OK, so now we have a name and time period. Do we go to the house with this? His name, and start talking to him? "

"No, let's see if there's anything in the old newspapers about him. I think we still need to investigate more. See if there's a reason he is in that house. If it's him."

A few hours later, after searching through every internet site she could find, they had an obituary of Alton Pacetti:

## THE EVENING RECORD

St Augustine, Florida

Thursday, 1901

Alton R Pacetti, life-long resident of this section of Florida, residing on Saragossa St, died Thursday night in a freak accident at his home, in St. Augustine. Funeral services were held Sunday afternoon at 3 o'clock at Pellicer Creek Cemetery.

Mr. Pacetti is survived by a wife, four sons, Ellis, Lee, Alton Jr and Jack, two daughters, Mrs. W. M. Miller of Savannah Ga. and Mrs. Carter of St. Johns County, also several brothers and sisters.

In the passing of Mr. Pacetti, another pioneer of Florida is lost. He and his relatives were among the first settlers in this part of Florida. The Pacetti's are descendants of the original French Huguenots who settled in large numbers along the coast in the early part of the fifteenth century.

"I wonder what kind of freak accident. He might not even know he's dead." Lilly said. "You know, he might be seeing these people in his house, and think they are robbing him or something. I bet you anything, he really doesn't know he's dead!" She could hear the excitement in her on voice. They sat for a minute reading the obituary again. Trying to see if they might be able to piece some of the mystery together.

"We aren't going to learn anything new here. I think we should just go to the house and take it from there." Beck looked at her sisters. There was doubt and fear on their faces. But in the end, they agreed to go.

"I need to leave a note for the girls, hold on a sec."

"Why not have them all meet here and we can have dinner after?"

"That works, I'll get something out of the fridge." Lilly walked to the kitchen.

"I'll call the girls and tell them to all come here after school and work. I'll meet you in the car." Sher said to Beck.

Beck waiting for Lilly and Sher to come out to the car. When they did, she asked

"Should we take anything with us?"

"You already doused the house with salt right?" Sher snickered at her.

"Hey, I was trying to protect your ass. And mine."

"I think we should just go, and see if we can get him to talk to us." Lilly said with an even and level tone. No fear,

48

no stress. She felt very calm. As if she were on her way to the store, or school to drop the girls off. She felt a deep calm. And knew her heritage was coming back to her. Not in full force. But coming back all the same. And it was a welcome feeling. She had hidden this side of herself for so long, she had forgotten how intimate it felt. She could feel the warmth inside her spreading through out her body. Her ears and cheeks flushed. Her hands tingled. And she looked at Beck and Sher, who were also staring at her, and smiled. A brilliant peaceful smile.

"You ok?" Beck asked.

"Never better. And soon, very soon, I will be able to say that all the time."

"Glad you're back Lil." Sher said and hugged her. "Now let's go ghost busting!"

# *Nine*

They climbed the steps of the house and eased open the door. The salt was apparent on the threshhold of the doors. As they stepped across the threshhold, nothing happened. But they could feel and sense the turmoil within the house.

"He's pretty pissed off Beck." Lilly said. They made their way to the kitchen and sat at the table. "I say we cast a circle, do a séance and see what he wants to tell us."

"Do we even need to do all that?" Lilly questioned. "Seems like we can just start talking and see where it leads us."

"I'm a firm believer in rather be safe than sorry. We cast a circle and he can't get to us, nothing can. We just start interacting with him, and we are at his mercy. Let's cast, that's my vote." Beck answered as she looked around the house.

"Then you better do it quick, because I'm getting a feeling he's been building up strength since we left him, I don't think he's gonna be held for much longer." Beck took charge from there. Lilly hadn't cast a circle in years and Sher liked to sit and watch. Beck was the strongest when it came to this part. So she poured the salt, and began her casting started in East,

"I call to the power of air, we ask that you watch over us in our circle." As she called to each, she faced the direction in compass. East, South West and North. "I call to Fire, we ask that you watch over us within this circle. I call to water, we ask that you watch over us within this circle. I call to earth, we ask that you watch over us within this circle." She then lit three candles. One for the Gods, one for the Goddess and one for unity. As she sat, she saw Sher looking at her.

"What?" Beck asked her.

"That was fast, I know there's a lot more to that."

"I thought that I'd do it quickly, considering."

"Works for me."

"And it worked for him too." Lilly said. Both women looked in the direction Lilly pointed.

"How long has he been there Lilly?"

"I'd say as long as it took for you two to poke fun at Beck's casting. He's just been standing there. I don't know that he knows we are here. He seems to be looking for something. He looks like he's crying."

The man looked around the kitchen. As if he was searching for something. He took no notice of the women sitting at the table. He walked to the window and looked out. His mouth was moving as if he were talking. But no sound came from him. You could see on his face the irritation. Something or someone was making him mad. They couldn't get a good look at his face. He seemed to come and go. But what they could see were lines from father time. And hard work. He gestured with his hands with every movement from his mouth. But still there was no sound.

"Should we try and talk to him, or just watch him?" Lilly couldn't take he eyes off him. She knew that ghosts and spirits were hard pressed to materialize, but this man seemed to be so real that she could touch him. She stood without warning and reached for him.

"Lilly!" Both sisters grabbed for her at once. "You can't go out of the circle"

51

"I, I don't know why I tried that. I know to stay here. But I just want to touch him, he seems so sad."

"That's not our time Lily, outside of this circle. If you step out before I close it, well, you know what might happen. So, just don't, OK, just let this play out and see if there's anything we can learn from him."

"I think we will be able to help, Lilly, just wait though."

"Lilly, look at him, is he the man from the Historical Society?"

"I can't see his face really. If he would just turn around, "

And he did. Lilly sucked in her breath. He was the man she had seen before. Only he seemed to have aged. His eyes were hollow and his face was gaunt.

"It's him. He is changing. He looked younger when I first saw him. Now he looks so old."

"Try and talk to him Lilly."

"What do I say?" Lilly asked as they watched the man's anger grow.

"Ask him his name or, I don't know, what year it is, or what's he so mad at."

Lilly looked at her sister, all those questions seemed odd to her. She looked at the man, and then asked him.

"Can I help you?" He didn't seem to hear her. He did not react to her voice at all.

"What are you doing here?" She tried again. And she stood up. Both Sher and Beck reached for her.

"I'm not going out side the circle. Relax. I just want to see if I can make him see me." She turned to him. He did see her. He was looking at her with hatred in his eyes. He saw her, but not her. The air seemed to weigh her down. He stepped closer to her. He saw someone from his time standing there. There was something about him that made her want to reach out and touch him. She saw the hate, the anger. But she felt no fear. He moved closer still. And she slowly moved to him. She reached out her hand to him, but there was no touch. Her fingers went through him.

"Why have you done this to me Isabella?" His tone was a mix of hurt and ruthlessness. His voice startle Lilly.

"I'm not Isabella." Lilly said to him. "My name is Lilly."

He just glared at her. He turned to face the sink and clutched the sides of the counter. His knuckles turned white with the pressure.

"What have I done to you to make to find another bed to occupy? I work for you, I help you with our children. I give you everything you ever asked me for. I'm adding onto this house for you. You wanted a bigger house, and I'm giving it to you. But you're still not happy. What is it you want? What more can I do for you?"

He turned to her again. This time it was not anger or hate in his face. This time it was anguish. His wife had cheated on him. And he loved her still.

"Tell me Isabella, tell me what to do to make you love me again."

"I'm not, I'm not Isabella." Lilly stammered. She stepped closer to him still.

"He's not listening to me," Lilly said to Sher and Beck. "Or he can't hear me." Lilly turned to look at her sisters. Their mouths were moving, but she heard no sound. And in an instant, she realized, she'd stepped across the salt. She was in his world now, his time. She tried to come back into the circle. Just before she stepped across to re join them, she stopped. If she stepped back, would she be able to help him? Would she bring him to their world then? Would she bring something back across the salt line with her? She had to play this out. She had to stay outside the circle long enough to help him. To put him at peace.

She turned to her sisters, and reached out to touch Beck, her fingers went through her.

"Damn it!" Both Sher and Beck could still see her, this much she knew. They were both staring at her. But could they hear her. She held Beck's gaze. Trying to give her a 'look' that would let her know what she was going to try and do. Beck reached out for Sher's hand, and gave Lilly a nod. So she did understand her intentions.

When Lilly turned back to the ghost, he was headed out of the kitchen and through the living room. When Lilly stated to follow, something inside her broke. She felt as if her body had been pulled in two parts. She looked back towards the kitchen table, now she saw was a stranger sitting between Beck and Sher. And by the looks of it, they did not see her. This must be Isabella Lilly thought. And instantly disliked her. She lingered in the kitchen to see if she could get a feel for Isabella. Maybe she would be able to find out why she had cheated.

Isabella walked to the sink and started to wash some dishes.

"I don't love you any more Alton, I just don't love you. I don't think I ever did." She said softly. Lilly heard the front door slam shut. She was about to follow him out when Isabella turned. There was no remorse on her face. There was no hurt or love lost. She had a look of a woman who was used to being pampered. Spoiled. A woman who wanted more, no matter what she was handed.

"So, why did you cheat on him Isabella?" Lilly knew she would get no answer.

Isabella started up the stairs and Lilly followed her. She went to the nursery and picked up a crying baby. She then went to what had been her and Alton's room and lay down with him.

Lilly stayed in the corner of the room. Hoping to hear more from Isabella. Minutes ticked away and Lilly thought she and the baby had fallen to sleep. She was about to go back down the stairs to her sisters when a loud crash came from over head. She could hear Alton yelling and several more bangs. Abruptly, she saw a shadow fall from the roof and cling to the window sill.

"Help me Bella, help me in?" Alton was hanging onto the window sill, with gloved hands.

Isabella rushed to the window and grabbed a hold of his wrists.

"Pull me up, hurry, God hurry!"

Lilly wanted desperately to help, but knew she couldn't. And then it happened. She watched as Isabella loosened her grip. She stared at her husband. There was no look of hate or any emotion at all. She simply let him go.

"What are you doing, for god's sake! Help me! Help me!"

She said nothing. She backed away from the window and watched him try and pull himself up. But the gloves slipped. He couldn't get a good hold.

"Please Isabella, Ill give you a divorce if you want, just please, help me!"

Still she stood watching him, not moving to help. Again, minutes ticked by. Alton feverishly tried to gain control. But his gloves prevented him from doing so.

And then he was gone. She thought his scream could be heard she thought for miles. Isabella didn't move. She didn't run to the window or down the stairs. She stood still. When she turned towards Lilly, there was no emotion on her face. A few seconds later she laid back on the bed with her child. Lilly ran to the window, when she looked out she saw nothing. No body. No man who fell to his death.

"He made it." She whispered. "He didn't die from the fall"

She turned to run down the stairs only to see Beck and Sher watching her.

"We broke the circle when we heard you screaming" Beck said to her. She could see fear and concern on both their faces.

"Scream? I wasn't screaming."

"Yes you were Lilly. That's why we broke the circle. To come see what happened. Are you ok? What was going on? What did you see?"

She told them what Isabella had done. And how Alton had pleaded with her for help. Help that she did not give.

"No wonder he's still here and pissed off. He must think that Joan, or any woman is Isabella. And as far as he knows, he's still alive. He's coming back to her to confront her about not helping him. That's got to be it." Sher said to them.

"Ok, so now how do we let him know he's really dead. And that it's been over a hundred years since?" Lilly asked.

They walked back to the kitchen and sat down again. Lilly laid her head on the table and breathed deeply.

"I feel for him you know. He loved her. You could see it on his face when he was here in this room talking to her. When he was hanging outside that window, Gods I wanted to help him. The fear in his voice. I don't know how she could do that to him. Her husband. I know the feeling of hating your husband and wanting to get rid of him, but she murdered him."

# *Ten*

They sat in silence. Absorbing what hey knew. Trying to think of ways to help the ghost, the man, come to peace.

"I think we might need to do more than cast a circle. I think we might need to do a séance. See if we can call to him and try and explain to him that he's dead. So that he can move on."

"What do we need for a full séance?" It was Lilly who asked. She knew there was no waiting now. She was thrust into this head first and there was no time to try and get used to it, or come back to her magic a little at a time.

"We need to do this now," Lilly said out loud. "He's been here too long, he needs peace."

"I'll get the candles." Beck told her.

Beck left the house to get the items they would need from her car. She always came prepared.

"You sure you are up to this Lilly? We can wait a night, he's been here this long, twenty four hours won't make much difference to him.

"I'm ok." She said absently. "Do you think he relives that? Do you think that every day he goes through that all over again?"

"I don't know, he could be stuck in a loop. When we do the séance, we will be able to find out, I think. Or, at least, talk with him.

"Are you sure you're ok, you look kind of out of it."

"Yes, I'm fine. I'm just tired I think. And shocked, I just witnessed a murder from a hundred years ago." They both laughed nervously. Beck came back with a basket filled with candles of every color, and some more salt.

"OK, I think I have everything that we need. Lilly, you really up for this?"

"Yeah, I'm good. Beck, do you think he's stuck in a loop?"

"Yes, sorry, but yes I do. I think he's reliving this over and over. But for what's its worth, I don't think *he* knows it. This is the last thing he remembers, and it was painful to him. He died, but he doesn't really know that. We need to tell him, and send him away. Maybe when we do that, he will find some peace." Beck set her candles on the table, and opened her book. A Book of Shadows her gran told them. They all had one of their own. In which they wrote down rituals to the Gods and Goddess of their choosing. Beck fell to the Greek Gods though she knew them all. They kept memories in them as well. What chants worked best with which ritual. What herbs helped ailments. The books read like scrap books. Not the normal Book of Shadows. They had herbs they dried taped or glued to the pages. Pictures of events and ritual alters. Their book told their story of magic and life. Each as different as the sister that owned it.

"I'm amazed you are handling this so well, Lilly. Considering." Sher said as she sat next to her. Lilly looked at Sher and sat back in her chair.

"Do I have a choice? If I freak out now, who helps him? You both said this is going to take the three of us. So, if I don't think about it to much right now, I can do it. If you make me think too much on it, I will freak out, I promise you that. And for the record, I will think about this after we are done, and one of you will be staying with me tonight. "Lilly smiled at her sisters.

They had the salt poured and sage burning. Sweet grass for extra cleansing.

"This is going to be a simple chant, I don't have a lot of stuff, and it feels like we are running out of time. His energy is escalating, let's do a simple chant, ok with you two?' Both Sher and Lilly nodded their heads and Beck began.

She said the chant three times and sat silent as they waited holding hands. And the air became thicker. The lights dimmed and the candles flickered.

"All the hair on my body just stood up. And I can guess by the looks on your faces, he is behind me at the sink again. Why the hell did I sit here?!" Beck sighed.

"Ok he's back and I am starting to feel his anger again." Lilly uttered. She watched him as he kept his back to them. This time when he turned, he looked at them.

"Who are you?" He asked.

Lilly stood, not letting go of her sister's hands, she didn't want to loose herself again.

"My name's Lilly, this is Sher and Beck."

"Are you here to see Isabella, she was just here, she should be back in a minute. I reckon she's out back right now."

"No, we are here for you Alton. We are here to help you."

"Me?" He looked at all three women in turn. His face showed confusion. Lilly noticed this time she could see lines on his face. Aged lines from years of hard work and worry. But handsome. His clothes were worn and torn in several places. His hands were the hands of a man who knew how to work. He was no pencil pusher. His shoulders were wide and straight and you could see the muscled arms through his shirt. The buttons were pulled tight.

"Alton," Lilly started "I don't know how to tell you this, or ease into this story." She looked to Sher for help.

"What do you remember about today Alton?"

"I don't understand what you're talking about, what do I remember from a day that's not done?" He asked.

"You were here, in this room when you confronted your wife about her affair." His eyes opened wide. And then relaxed again. He was trying not to let them see the hurt. He thought Isabella had told these women about her affair. Snickering behind his back.

"Isabella did not tell us this Alton. We know this because, well, because you are haunting this house. You are stuck on this day, a loop, and you are reliving this over and over. And you're hurting the women who live here, thinking that they are Isabella." Beck said abruptly.

"I'm what?" And now it was his turn to snicker. "I'm sorry ladies, but I think you have the wrong house. I've lived here all my life and my pa did too. What? You said I'm haunting this house? Then you must think I'm dead. But, if I'm dead, how am I talking to you?" He stepped closer to the sisters. He reached for Beck's shoulder, and his hand went through it. His face lost the playfulness it had just seconds before. And he tried to touch her again. He slowed his hand down as he reached for her. As if he knew what they said was true. But he tried anyway. Once again, his hand went through her shoulder. He looked at each woman in turn.

"I'm dead then." There was no question in his voice. He knew. He turned to the sink again and looked out the window.

"How long?"

Lilly answered "I think over a hundred years." Her voice was hardly more then a whisper. Her heart felt for this man. This ghost. She knew the things he had done to others over the last hundred years. But she also knew he thought he was coming for Isabella.

"So, she succeeded in letting me die. She let me fall from that window and I died. I'm dead and she lived. Did she marry him? She must be dead now too. But did she marry him?" He turned to them. But they had no answers for him.

"We don't know," Beck told him. "We just are here to help you move on. Give you peace. To help you let go and move on. So that the woman who owns this house can come home. You have frightened a lot of women over the past hundred years, Alton. It's time for you to go." The words from Beck were harsh. But her tone was soft.

"Can you make this right? Can you make sure my family knows what she did to me? I want them to know what she did. She let me fall from that window. She stood right there and let me fall to my death. I want my family to know that!" His anger was coming through to them. Lights flickered, the air became heavy and thick. The smell of death hung in the air.

"Alton, you must calm down" Sher was trying to tell him. "We will do what we can for you, to help your family know what happened. But you have to relax. Do you see a way out of this house? Like a light or something?" Beck and Lilly looked at her. She shrugged her shoulders. They were not sure if they believed in heaven, but with all the "Go into the light" stuff they heard about, she thought she'd try it with him.

"You mean a light to heaven?"

"Yes, something like that."

"I see nothing, no light, nothing. Just the three of you, and you're fading."

He was fading from them. His voice was not so loud and his features not so real now. He was turning back to the ghost that haunted this house for over a hundred years. They watched as his disappeared completely from them. And felt the change in the air around them as well. He was gone. At peace they all hoped. With the last of his strength, they heard a faint 'thank you'.

They looked at each other and sat in silence. All of them gathering up their nerves to talk about what they had just witnessed. But as the minutes went by, no one had the courage to talk. They blew out the candles, opened the circle and swept the salt from the floor. As they drove to Lilly's, the silence still hung between them, unbroken.

In Lilly's kitchen they sat as she pored them all a glass of wine. She sat between them.

"So," Sher began "What the hell was that? I mean, really, did that just happen?"

"I think we are a lot stronger than we thought. Unless you two have done this before and not bothered to tell me about it." Lilly looked at both her sisters and knew that wasn't true. They were just as stunned as she was.

"I think we should charge for this." Beck said, and with that, the three of them burst out with laughter.

# *Eleven*

Over the next few days life ran pretty regularly. No new ghosts to attend to. The girls pretty much had settled into their new lives. Each making friends and enjoying school. As much as teenagers can. Lilly had applied to the college in town for an art position. She had an interview at the end of the week. On Saturday morning Lilly and her daughters were planning a day of shopping. They all needed costumes for Beck's party next week and the plans were to hit the Jacksonville mall. They all were excited to get out of the house and think about something fun. Something other then school or work.

As Lilly sat on the back porch drinking her coffee and reading the morning paper, Stephanie came out to join her.

"When did you start drinking coffee, Steph?" Lilly asked.

"Since I started college courses in high school."

Steph never was a morning person. So Lilly waited for her to talk next.

"What time do you want to go today" Steph asked her.

"Whenever you three get ready is fine with me. Aunt Sher told me of a few shops to go to. When we find what we want, we can have lunch too."

"There's a store at Five Points that Cathy told me about. Her mom's all into pirates and stuff. There's a group in town that has parties all the time. Maidens Pub I think it's called. We can start there, and might not have to make a day of it."

"Sounds good to me. Whenever you all are ready."

"Mom," Steph's voice held a note of apprehension. This made Lilly listen to her with more then her ears.

"Have you heard from Dad?"

Lilly knew before she asked what her question would be.

"No honey, I haven't. Have you girls?"

"No, he hasn't called me. He hasn't called any of us. I know Savannah has called him every day since we left. But he hasn't returned any of her calls. It's like we don't exist any more. Do you think he is mad at us for coming with you?"

"I don't know, honey. I'm sorry to put you girls through this. If you want me to, I'll call him and see if I can find out why he hasn't called." Though it was the last thing Lilly wanted to do. She really didn't care if she ever talked with Steve again. For all she cared, he could get hit by a Mack truck. But her daughters did care. So she would make the call if they wanted her to.

"Do you think he will answer for you?"

"I don't know, he might." But she knew he would. Because he was waiting for her to call and beg to come back. Or tell him life was too hard out here with out him. She would never tell him that. Even if it did get hard. Crawling back to him would never happen. She had Sher and Beck. They would never let her fall, never let her have to make that call to him.

They spent two hours in a costume shop in Five Points. Trying on several different outfits each. And not all of them Pirate. They tried on clown outfits and fell into fits of laughter. To Lilly it was music. When the girls started laughing together, it was unstoppable. And why would she want to. She watched them. Trying costumes on and making silly faces and acting out funny scenes. The shop owner was getting a laugh from them too.

"Those all your girls?" She asked

"Yep. All three of them are mine." Lilly had a smile from ear to ear. They were acting out some spy movie they all had seen several times.

"Your house must be a riot all the time." She said, also smiling. "Contagious, that kind of laughter." She made her way back to the front of the store to help another customer.

"Ok girls, what are we getting today?"

When they went through all the choices, they all settled on different looks.

"Mom, where's your costume?" Sarah asked. The three girls looked at her.

"Mom, you have to get a costume."

"I think the three of you took all she had. I can figure something out."

"No, that's not fair." Savannah said. And her eyes started to fill with tears. "Mom, you have to get one to!"

"Don't worry honey, I'll just get something from a different store. It's Halloween, there are costumes all over." She hugged Savannah close to her. She knew her youngest daughter wore her heart on her sleeve. If she thought that Lilly was being left out of something, she wouldn't have any more fun.

"Yeah, but they are the cheap ones. You need to get a real one like ours." Savannah looked to her oldest sister, pleading with her to fix it.

"I bet if we ask, the owner might have something in the back that we could look at. It might be old and need of repair. But mom you can sew really well, right?" She could see all her girls were starting to panic now.

"Ok, let's ask if she has something in the back. And we can go from there, ok?"

They went to the front of the store and asked the owner for another costume.

"You know, I have a few things I was planning on taking off the shelf. They just weren't rented very often, but come around back and let's have a look."

She showed them a trunk that had several older costumes.

"These were here when I bought the store. I guess 10 years now. I don't know how long they have been here before. They had some good use from them. If you find something, you can have it. No charge. I was just gonna throw them out anyhow.' She went back up front and Lilly and the girls looked at each other.

"Ok, let's open this up and see what we've got."

The trunk was old. You could tell by the look of it. Ornate, with large clasps that locked. Neither was. The keys were sure to have been long since lost. The grain told a tale of age. The coloring was dark. And the smell of old wood was slight.

When Lilly cracked the top open, the smell of moth balls struck them. They all expected bugs to run out. But nothing did.

"How long have these been here?" Sarah asked.

"Didn't she say she just put these away? Looks like they have always been in this trunk." Steph said.

Lilly pulled the first of two dresses from the trunk. "I thought they were pirate outfits?' Savannah asked. "This is a dress."

And it was a dress. A dress like none of them had ever seen. Heavy material with lace and brocade. Gold and cream colors. Lilly pulled it from the box and could feel a change in the air. She couldn't help herself. She held it up in front of her and walked to the mirror. She turned left and right and imagined herself in it.

"Try it on Mom." They said in unison.

She closed the curtain behind her and began to change. When she emerged from the changing room, the three girls gasped.

"Mom, you look like a bride." Savannah said.

"No, you really look like you belong to that time." Steph told her. They all gathered around the mirror to look at their mother.

"You look so different." Sarah told her.

"That's because we are used to seeing mom in jeans and tee shirts. With messy hair and no make up. I think you're beautiful, and with a brush and some eye liner, imagine what we can do to you!" Steph was excited to see her mom like this. They were all used to seeing their mom, as a mom. But now, with just a dress on, they saw her as a woman, like their eyes had opened for the first time to see that their mom was human too. That she was real.

They stood there, looking at Lilly for nearly fifteen minutes. No one talking, no one laughing. All stuck in their own thoughts.

"I don't look much like a pirate with this on though. Is there anything else in that trunk?" Even Lilly had a hard time turning away from her reflection.

"No, there are a few more dresses, but none like this one. I think you should take this and wear it for the party. No one will recognize you in this Mom." Steph walked to the trunk and began to close the lid. "I wonder if we can have the trunk too?"

"Yes, you can have the trunk and every thing that's in it." The shop owner told them. With a nervous laugh. Lilly heard the strain in her voice. But couldn't figure out why.

"Are you sure" She asked. "It looks awful old, like an antique. Are you sure you want to get rid of this. It's so beautiful." Excitement came to her eyes. As if she were a child on Christmas morning getting just what she asked Santa for. But why Lilly wondered? Why would she be so happy to rid herself of such a beautiful and old trunk like this? The girls were excited too. But in a much different way. The dress and trunk for free. That was their excitement. Thinking they were getting away with something. As if the shop keeper didn't know the quality of the items. As if she didn't understand the expense of what she was losing. But the more Lilly watched her, the more she wondered what was wrong with the dress and trunk. A chill ran down her. And a whisper of dread came about her.

They loaded the trunk, the dress, and the pirate costumes in the back of the jeep. They walked across the street to an Italian restaurant and ate lunch. All the while Lilly couldn't shake the chill she had in the store. When she looked out to the costume shop, she saw the owner looking at them, smiling. As if she had a secret.

They walked the length of Five Points and headed home. It was almost 3pm by the time they pulled into the drive. All the girls grabbed their costumes and went to their rooms. To re-try them on and to call friends and tell about the mysterious trunk they now had in the middle of the dining room. Lilly herself wasn't sure what to do with it. Maybe in the front room of the house. The room that used to be called the parlor. That seemed right to her. Old name for an old trunk. She pulled the dress out and took it to her own room and hung it up. With out another thought to the dress, she went on with her day.

# Twelve

"So, I hear you scored at Five Points last weekend." Beck said.

"Yeah there's a really cool costume shop there. They had every kind of costume you can imagine. She even had an adult area. Only I didn't go in. We had a great time, the girls tried on a bunch of different things. They were so funny. I didn't think we'd ever get out of there. I was thinking that the clerk was gonna kick us out they where so loud. But she kinda joined in. I haven't laughed like that, God, I don't know when."

They meet tonight at Lilly's. Out on the front porch. Lilly and Sher sat in the swing that has been there since 1936. She loved this swing. They all did. As kids they would lay in it and push off from the house. Every now and then the swing would hit the side of the house and their grandma would come running to tell them to stop. This is the swing they played Tarzan on, the swing that on Friday nights, when the whole family met, they played music on. Uncles with guitars and friends with sweet voices. That swing that they watch the neighbors by. Popeye and Olive they called them. This porch held memories of Osteen's for three generations. And now it would start a fourth. Her daughters and nieces.

As they swung and talked the night air cooled. And the San Marco traffic eased. All the girls were there tonight as well.

Up stairs looking over the costumes and talking the normal teenage girl talk. School, boys, jobs, boys.

"You know," Lilly started "I did have a dream the other night about that dress. I can't remember it all, but it was something like the seller of the dress, or the maker. She was old and scary and was being cheated by the buyer. I can't see it but she was pissed off that she was getting screwed." She thought for another minute, but the dream was gone.

"OK, show us the dress and the trunk. I might be able to sell the trunk at the store if you want me to." Beck told her.

They went into the parlor where the trunk sat in the right front corner of the room. Lilly knelt next to it and opened it. As she did, and subtle wind blew through the sisters. Lilly stood up immediately. Grabbed for Becks hand, but shied away. They stood perfectly still. Hardly breathing. A grey, green light mist swirled out of the trunk and hovered above it.

"Lilly, where did the trunk come from?" Beck asked her, not moving. All of them stone still. The mist above the trunk was slow swirling. Changing from green to black and back again. The lights dimmed in the room, and throughout the house. They could hear the girls complaining and coming to the top of the stairs. Beck took a few steps back and held her hand out to stop them. All 9 stopped at once. As did their chatter. They quietly came down the stairs. Beck never took her eyes from the mist. It swirled and formed and swirled again. The air was full of electricity. Silence filled the house as they all watched a female form with in the mist.

She was beautiful. Her eyes were emerald green and her hair was a white blond. Her face became cleared as minutes ticked by. All the women in the house were silent. Lilly, Beck and Sher, not touching because they knew not to. If they did, the energy they put off would electrify the room and no telling what would happen. So they knew to stay clear from each other.

"Don't touch each other." Beck told her daughters and nieces. "Not in any way." She didn't look back at them on the stairs. She wouldn't take her eyes from the woman forming beside the trunk.

"Lilly, who is she?" Sher asked and a slight whisper. Her eyes glued to the form as well.

"I don't know, I think she's from the dreams I've been having."

"You mean night mare Mom. You are moaning at night. Since Saturday." Steph and Sarah said to her.

The woman formed and faded and formed and faded. Swirls of mist rose and fell as if she were breathing. Her eyes were hollow now. Never coming in clear as they did at first. Her dress was tan, or gold. The fabric looked as if it would be soft at the touch.

"Mom, I'm scared" Savannah said.

"Don't be" the three sisters said at the same time. Knowing at this moment, there was nothing to fear. "She can't hurt us, she can't even keep her own form." Lilly said.

But as Lilly said it, Sher and Beck and Lilly felt the cold fingers of dread climbed their necks. The three looked at each other. They spoke not a word. They didn't have to. They all saw what each one was thinking. Something was not right here. Something was wrong. Deadly wrong.

The feeling the three of them were getting was not one of happiness or comfort. Not one of a light heartedness. But one of pain and sorrow. A feeling of fear and anger. A mixture of despair and hate. Before it grew bigger, and stronger Beck decided this was enough. The feeling in the air was scaring her now as well.

"We need to do something quick here. We can't let her get her full power. We might not be able to handle her yet"

"Any suggestion on how to get her out of my house?"

"Just this" Sher said and walked up to the truck and slammed the lid shut. As the lid hit the trunk, a burst of hot wind stormed through the house. The windows rattling and the walls themselves were vibrating. A moan of anguish left their ears ringing.

Several minutes went by while no one breathed. No one spoke. They just stayed where they were and looked around the room. As if waiting for her to come back. They where. All were thinking she was going to return. They were right. But not for many nights.

# *Thirteen*

They had all gone to Sher's house. None of them wanted to stay alone. Sher and Beck and Lilly thought they needed to be together. Besides, they all had a lot to talk about. Lilly's daughters knew nothing of this side of their mom. They had never heard her talk of this gift she had. They had questions, which Lilly thought would be best answered by the three of them. When they had all settled down at Sher's, they met on the back porch. Sher had the largest house out of all the sisters. They would each have a room to sleep in, and their daughter's would flop where ever they wanted. Sher's three girls had their own rooms, so it was a good guess they would divide and sleep in threes.

When everyone was outside, Sher thought it time for her to tell her nieces the truth. She knew Lilly wasn't going to be able to start. So she opened the avenue to the girls herself. Her own daughters knew just about everything they needed to know. And tonight she figured it was time for them all to know the rest.

"So, anyone want to venture a guess at what we are?" She tried to be light about this. She didn't want to scare Savannah and Sarah and Steph.

"Um, let me take a guess, you're a witch." Steph said without much emotion.

Lilly didn't know what to say to the girls. She didn't know how to start this conversation. She knew one day she might have to. But the more she put it off, the harder it got to tell them.

"Well, I don't know that a witch is the right term. But we can do a few extra things that normal people cant." Beck said. She could feel the tenseness from Steph. And wanted to ease her before she started to feel as if Lilly had betrayed her.

Lilly saw and felt it too. That's when she decided to stop hiding behind her sisters and face her daughters head on.

"You know, witch is a good term for what we can do. That's what the Osteen women have been called for century's now. So let's call a spade a spade." She held her head up a bit higher, washing the shame from herself. She looked each daughter in the eye.

"Your mom's a witch. And both of your aunts are too. As is your cousin and yourselves, I bet. I've never known this gift we have to skip a generation. So I'm sure you three have some skills." She waited. Her three daughters were staring at her. She waited for their anger.

"Holy Shit mom, are you joking?" Was what came first from Sarah. Then Steph relaxed and grinned from ear to ear at her.

"That's pretty cool mom."

Before she knew it, she was smiling herself.

"What's Aunt Lilly's specialty?" Cleo asked her mom in a whisper.

"She can feel the emotions of the spirit." Sher answered.

"You feel the ghost?" Savannah asked Lilly.

"I can't feel the ghost honey, but I can feel the emotions it has. Happiness, sadness, confusion and anger. Are you ok, Savannah?" The girls quieted down. Out of all her girls,

Savannah was the most likely to have a problem with this news. She was the daughter most like her. Her heart was worn on her sleeve. She ached for anyone who hurt and cried with anyone who was sad. She was the kind of kid who took sandwiches' to the homeless on the street. She was the one she worried most about. And she was still her baby.

"I don't know Mom. Everyone thinks this is so cool. I don't want to be the only one who thinks it's wrong. Not wrong really, just, I don't know." Lilly held out her hand for her daughter to take. And she did. With that gesture, Lilly knew she would be ok with all that was happening.

"So all of you can do something different? When it comes to spirits?" Sarah asked her mom and her aunts.

"Yes, I feel their emotions, Aunt Sher can see them and Aunt Beck can hear them. And when we all touch each other, we get it all."

"So why didn't you tell us this before?" they all asked at once.

"Because your dad didn't like it and I tried to make it go away."

The three girls looked to their aunts and cousins, "You all knew?' Steph asked.

"Yeah" said Rory

"But we weren't supposed to talk about it 'til your mom said something to you first." Cybele told them. Kinda a hard secret to keep. Considering."

"Considering what?" Savannah asked.

Cybele and Steph looked at each other, then at their moms.

"We all have a gift." Beck said to them.

Lilly watched the girl's faces for the understanding to take place. And it did. All at once.

"We have it too?" They asked in unison.

"Yes, I don't know who has what, but I can venture a guess." Lilly said to them

"What if we don't want it?' Sarah said. Looking down at her hands. Embarrassed that she didn't want a gift like her mother.

"Then you'll have to continue to block it out, like you have been doing." Sher said to them.

"Or, you can accept it, and let me tell you something," Cybele and Calista looked at each other, then at Steph and Sarah and Savannah. "It's pretty cool when you get it under control."

"I know that this is a lot to take in at once. But we are going to have to. Because, unfortunately, I have brought it to our house."

"No, you didn't, Lilly. Well yes technically you did. But you were tricked I think by the woman who owns that shop. I think that that is the first place we need to look. We need to ask her few questions." Beck said.

"Mom, I think she knew what she was doing when she said we could have everything in that trunk." Steph said to Lilly.

Everyone in the room agreed. Lilly sat back and looked to the sky for a minute.

"You know, I knew that when we came back here, things were going to be different for us. But I never thought that this was going to happen so fast. I mean I thought I might dabble in it again and start a few rituals. Get out the rust and all. But this is faster then I thought things would happen. First the man on Saragossa, what ten days ago. And now this? Who is she and what the hell is she doing in that trunk. And what time period is she in?"

"I don't know," said Cybele, Sher's oldest daughter. "But it looks like those clothes in that trunk were taken right out of the movie Pirates of the Caribbean. That dress that you have Aunt Lil has got to be identical to the one, what's her name, something Swan."

"Elizabeth, its Elizabeth Swan, and holy shit you're right!" Rory said. She turned to Beck and asked "Do you still have that movie Mom?" As she asked, she got up from the chair and started inside. "Come help me look Steph and Cyb."

The conversation grew from there. But it was easy. The tension was gone once the girls knew her secret. And with as hard as it was to talk about it, it was just that easy for her daughters to accept it. She felt guilt for a brief few minutes for not telling them sooner. For not giving them enough credit to handle what she had to tell. And for loving her just the same. None of them made her feel ashamed. Not like Steve had.

As the night drifted, the girls all made their way to bed. Slower, the last three, the oldest daughters went up as well.

"You don't mind staying tonight, do you Rowan?" Beck asked.

"No, I don't have any other plans and I don't have school tomorrow either. So it's cool. See you in the morning."

"Good night."

Lilly sighed. Closed her eyes and could feel her sisters stare. "Don't worry, I'm not going to come unglued." She said to them. Her eyes closed still. "I guess I'm driving to Five Points tomorrow and see what she knows."

# *Fourteen*

The next morning Lilly and Sher drove to five points only to find it closed.

"Maybe she opens at 9." Lilly said.

"Let's go get some coffee and come back and wait for her. It will give us some time to figure out what to ask her anyway."

At nine the 'closed' sign flipped to 'open' and they went it.

"I knew you'd be back. I thought I had more time, but I knew you'd be back to ask about the ghost."

"Why didn't you tell me first?" Lilly asked her.

"I couldn't, if you knew what came with that trunk, you would never have taken it. I can't keep it anymore. And you can't return it to me, I won't take it back." Her eyes grew large and scared with the thought of having the trunk back. But they didn't know why yet.

"OK, so I have this trunk now, with the little extra ghost attached to it. Can you tell me who she is? And what she wants? And maybe how to get rid of her?"

"I don't know." Was all she said at first. But you could see she knew a lot more then she was going to tell them.

"Now wait a minute," Sher said, "You know a lot about that trunk and I see no reason for you not to tell us. We can't bring it back, so what's the harm?"

"Listen, it's yours now, you deal with it. I'm out of it now. You took it, you took it. I didn't make you take it." She was nervous. Her eyes started to peer around the shop. As if she was looking for some one or something to help her, or hurt her.

"I don't want to give it back, I just want to know what you know about it. That's it." Lilly was getting mad now. Thinking that maybe she was putting her kids in harm with that trunk in the house.

She walked over to the shop keeper, trying to calm herself down.

"Wait, just wait. I'm Lilly and this is my sister Sher. What's your name?" She didn't answer, just looked at Lilly.

"It can't hurt for you to give us your name. I'm sure I can walk next door and ask what your name is, so just tell me your name so we can talk."

"Margo, my name's Margo Turner. And you're right, I need to tell you what I know. Just give me a minute to get myself together." She turned around, with her back to them, and steadied herself with the counter. After several deep breathes she turned to face them, once again.

"Let's go in the back, I'll make some coffee and I'll tell you all I know." She turned the open sign to closed and they followed her to the back and found a cute room with a small table and chairs. Margo filled the coffee maker and pulled creamer from the refrigerator. She pulled down three cups and sugar and invited Sher and Lilly to sit.

"Don't know where to begin. You know I have owned this costume shop for ten years. I bought it with all my savings. I thought this was going to be the best little costume shop ever. I had researched this store for two years before I bought it. I worked here too. Sheila, the woman who owned it before me, always seemed so happy and her finances were so great.

She never seemed to want for anything. That trunk was in the back the entire time I worked here. I never asked her what was inside. I never even took a peek myself. When she decided to sell, I couldn't move fast enough. I think it took less then a week before we agreed on the price. Three more weeks and we closed. She handed me the keys and said "It's all your'ss now Margo, good luck to you." And laughed. It wasn't until I asked her about the trunk that I remembered her laugh. It was sinister. I didn't ask her about the trunk. She said it was mine now. I bought it with the shop. Ok, I thought, no big deal. I opened it and looked through it. Loved the dress, tried it on, and out she came. I thought I was dreaming. I thought that I had too much to drink, or something. But there she was, so beautiful at first. Her eyes and hair, so perfect. It was like she didn't see me at first. But when she did…" Margo dropped her head into her hands and began to cry. Lilly and Sher both put a hand on her shoulder. "She took on a different form. She wasn't beautiful any more. She was ugly and grotesque. Her voice was a shrill cry. And the smell. Every day the same thing. Every night the screaming and crying over and over. I can't sleep, I have lost about 15 pounds. I don't date, my family never comes over. I love the costume shop. I won't give it up. And I'm so sorry for what I've done to you. I just saw you, and thought you looked strong enough to deal with her. I'm just not, not any more, not after ten years. I thought if I put the dress back and closed the lid, she'd stay inside. She did for a while. But soon she got stronger. I never heard from Sheila again. So I really don't know more then what I told you."

Lilly and Sher sat back in their chairs looking at Margo and then each other. There was nothing more for them to learn from her. Not that they knew much to begin with.

"Margo, while she haunted you, could you customers see or hear her?"

"I don't think so, no one ever said anything. But my customers mostly come at Halloween. And things are supposed to be scary then, right?"

After they left, and started to drive home to St Augustine, Lilly finally asked, "So what do we do?"

"I think its going to take opening that trunk again and see if we can speak to her."

"Yeah, I was afraid you were going to say that."

# *Fifteen*

In the office in Beck's store, the three sisters sat around the table, as Sher told Beck what they had found out through Margo.

"Its not much is it. There's not a name or time period to even go on. Or a city state, nothing." She got up and paced the small office. She had been in situations like this before. But nothing that felt so ominous, so dark. Her magic and Sher's was strong. But Lilly's was not. If something came out of that trunk that she wasn't ready for, there's no telling what they could open up. A vortex. If it turned out to be a vortex, she had no way of closing it. She had read about them. There was one in Ripley's. But not a lot of people knew that. The three of them had been there before, when they where teenagers.

"I don't think we should do this Beck. What if we get caught?" Lilly was the one who always worried. She wanted to have fun like her sisters. But she didn't want to get caught being bad. She wanted to be good. Like her mom was.

"Who is going to catch us? Besides, Tammy works here. If anyone says anything we can say we were coming to get her and got lost or something. Just relax and have fun. We aren't going to steel or trash the place. I just want to see if we can make contact with the ghosts here."

They met Tammy by the back door and she snuck them up to the third floor.

"Just be quiet for about 30 minutes and then you'll be alone here. If you get me into trouble for this Beck, I swear I'll kill you in your sleep." But with the harsh threat, Tammy was grinning wildly. She too wanted to make contact with the ghosts in the castle. But was too afraid to try.

"You better tell me everything tomorrow in first class. Shhh. I'll see you later." And she made her way down the stairs and into the manager's office.

Back and Sher and Lilly stayed completely still and quiet for the first thirty minutes, and then another fifteen for good measure.

"I think they are gone." Sher came out of her hiding place. And though the store was closed, it was not completely dark. They were able to see well enough around the building.

"This is kinda cool." Lilly said as she started to relax. They wandered around for about an hour looking at all the different artifacts. They made their way to the third floor and they could feel the heaviness in the air.

"She died up there," Beck said. She had like an apartment or something up there. They found her in the tub."

Sher lead the way to a room that faced the parking lot. On the corner of the building.

"Tammy says they call this room the vortex room."

She sat in the corner by the opening at the end of the hall. Sher and Lilly sat with her.

"Who are we looking to find here?"

"Ruth and Betty, they died in the fire in 1944. Only it wasn't by accident. They were murdered."

"How do you know that, Beck? As far as you know they died in that fire. Just like it says." But Sher knew it wasn't true. Her gran had talked to them about that fire. And all the things that were wrong with the reports.

Another hour drifted by with nothing more than a light hum from the air conditioner. The girls whispered about school and friends. About home work and grades. And boys that they liked. And girls that they didn't. For the most part they were inseparable. There were fights, as there are between sisters. But they were few and far between. And the unspoken trust between them and their mother let them do about anything they wanted. When the three were together, they didn't break the rules.

"Beck," Lilly whispered. "Beck there's something coming. I can feel it. Something in the hall."

"What is it Lilly, who is it?" Sher asked.

"I don't know, but it's not happy."

A minute later they heard a small sound. A tinking sound. The sound that a ring made on a banister.

"Do you hear that?' Beck asked them.

"I don't hear anything" Sher said.

Tink. Tink. Tink.

"I can hear his ring hitting the railing. That's the sound I hear."

"This is bad guys. This is bad. He's coming for this room. He's headed this way. And he is pissed!" Lilly said. Her whisper was filled with fear.

"Let's go, please Beck, lets go." Lilly said.

"Wait!" Sher said to her. "Wait just a minute. Let me look around the corner and see. Maybe it's something else." As she did Lilly jumped up. "He's here, its too late" was all she said. And she turned to Beck and grinned. A most evil grin.

"Grab her Sher, get her out of here. Hurry!" The both grabbed an arm of Lilly's and began to pull her from the room.

But before they could get out, a burst of hot air knocked them off their feet.

"He's here, and he's pissed. Why did she do it? Why won't she listen? If she would just listen to him, he wouldn't hurt her like that."

Sher and Beck grabbed at Lilly and drug her from the room. Down the hall and to the stairs. The whole while Lilly kept trying to stay on the third floor.

"Don't, let me go. I have to finish this."

"Just keep going Lilly, we have to get out."

They flew down the stairs with Lilly fighting them. Fortunately she was the smallest of the three and they were able to lift her off the floor. Before they made it to the door, she collapsed.

They pulled her from the building and sat with her. She was out for five minutes. When she came around she was frightened. And jumped up as if shocked.

"What the hell was that Beck? What was that?" Her eyes were large with a mixture of fear and furry.

"I'm sorry Lil. I didn't know that would happen."

"I want to go home, I don't want to go back in there."

"Ok, you can go. But I'm going back inside. I want to find out what happened, if I can." Beck told both Sher and Lilly.

"I'll go back in." Sher said. "Lil, you want to wait here for ma, or go home now?"

She didn't know. She wanted to run from the building. But she didn't want to be alone. She also had a small amount of curiosity that Sher and Beck had.

"I'll wait." She sat on the bench outside the entrance and waited. But not long

Beck and Sher made their way back to the third floor. With out Lilly the air didn't seem so tense. But it still held the feeling of danger.

"Sher, why did it affect Lilly like that?"

"I don't know. Unless it's her gift. She can feel the emotions. So I'd say that's it. He got a hold of her for that reason."

Without reason, Sher began to cry. While they walked through the entertainment room, she slid down the wall and sobbed. She looked at Beck and shrugged her shoulders.

"I don't know why I'm crying, but I feel so sad. So hurt. So betrayed." She folded her arms over her knees and laid her head on her arms. And sobbed. For ten minutes she cried. Beck sat with her and stroked her hair. Beck felt nothing. She didn't feel the anger nor the despair her sisters felt being here.

"I think we need to go. I'm sorry I brought you two here. I didn't know this would happen." Beck helped Sher up, hugged her, and lead her out of the building. When they reached the front doors she tuned, on the stairs was the silhouette of a woman. In her face was despair and grief. Beck turned to tell Sher, as she did the woman disappeared.

"There's not much choice, we can do it now, or tomorrow. Either way, we are gonna have to do something. Unless you want your house haunted by her."

"No thanks. I'd rather she leave. So, let's give me a break here, and do it after your party? I'd like to have some fun for a while and relax."

"Deal" Beck and Sher said at the same time.

86

# Sixteen

Saturday morning started like any other. She got her cup of coffee and sat on the back porch. Only today's back porch was still Sher's. She was soon joined by Sher and Cybele, then Steph.

"So, we still going tonight?" Steph looked at her mom.

"Yeah, we are going. I'm looking forward to it." Lilly said with her best smile on. Trying to cover the tiredness in her eyes.

"We are supposed to go to Aunt Beck's around noon. So we can help set things up. Mom and Aunt Lil can come later. Its kinda tradition for us to go over and help. With out the Moms." Cybele said to Steph.

"When can we go get our stuff?" Steph asked any one who had a car.

"You can drive in honey, when ever you want." Lilly told her. Knowing her daughter wanted to escape for a while. "Take you sisters and get some more things. Looks like we are camping out for a few more nights."

"Someone needs to call Rory and tell her not to come, she usually comes and gets everyone and shuttles them over. But I think Cybele or Steph can take them, you and I can go over later."

"That works for me. Anyone want breakfast?"

After the girls had left and Sher was busy with some computer work, Lilly showered and found herself on the back porch again. She loved this view of the marsh. Both Sher and Beck had great views of the marsh. She sat and laid back in the lounge chair hoping for a quick nap. But sleep would not come.

So she picked up her cell and made the dreaded call to Steve that she had put off since she and the girls came back to St. Augustine.

"Well, I knew I'd hear from you soon." Was how he answered the phone. Ready to beg to come back?"

"Hello to you to Steve and no, I'm not calling to come back. I'm calling to find out why you haven't called your daughters?' She held a monotone. She didn't want him to know she was mad that he hadn't called them. And she didn't want him to know he was affecting her through the girls.

"They can talk to me when you come back. Besides, why should I talk to them, they left too."

"Steve, they came with me because I'm their mom. They didn't really have a choice. Just because you are mad at me, don't punish them for it."

"I'll punish whom ever I please, Lil. Don't forget that. Don't call here and try and tell me what to do. If you're not coming home, we have nothing to talk about."

"Fine by me. Good Bye Steve." And she snapped her cell shut.

It wasn't two minutes later that it rang with Steve on the other end.

"Don't hang up on me you bitch!" And she snapped the phone shut again. And giggled. She smiled with the perverse feeling of joy she was getting by aggravating him. Again the cell phone rang.

"Hello." She said.

"You are trying my patience Lillianna. You've had your little vacation. Now I expect you back by Monday. I'm tired of this game you are playing." You could hear the anger turning to rage in his voice. And once again she was glad she had left him.

"Steve, I'm not coming back. Not Monday, not ever. You might want to find a lawyer Monday, that's what I will be doing. The only reason I called was for the girls. To tell you to please call them. They are caught in the middle and they miss their dad."

"You'll be back. You can't make it with out me. You need me. Who's going to pay your bills? Huh? Where are you going to get money from? Work? Who would hire you? You have no skills, the only thing you are is a mother and wife. That's all you know how to be. So, when the money runs out, you'll come back, and Ill make you beg, boy will I."

"I'm not coming back, again Ill say this slow so you can understand. I. WILL. NOT. BE. BACK." Snapping the cell shut for the last time, she turned off the ringer.

She wanted to throw it into the marsh. But loved the marsh to much to damage it. So she threw it against the side of the house. Twice. She felt better until she realized Sher was watching her.

"I take it that was the lovely Steve?"

"Yes, He thinks I'll come crawling back to him when the money runs out."

"Runs out? Doesn't he know that you transferred everything in your name?"

Lilly looked at Sher and a smile crept across her face.

"No. I didn't tell him and I don't think he's check yet. I took his name off my credit cards, so he couldn't cancel them.

And the money from gran, it was always in my name. So in truth, he will run out of money way before I do." Again she smiled at Sher.

"I'm proud of you Lil. You sneaky thing."

"I think I'm gonna need a really good lawyer though. When he does find out, he's gonna be really mad. I don't know what he will do." With that thought, the smile faded from her face. She knew better than anyone what he was capable of.

"No worries today. He can't do anything today. So, let's have some fun."

Sher and Lilly headed to Beck's around four that afternoon. Through out the day they talked and laughed, Sher careful not to mention Steve or the trunk. She knew Lilly needed a break, they all needed a break one way or another. And the party was perfect.

It was a party three fold. It was Becks birthday, Halloween and a full moon.

# *Seventeen*

When Lilly and Sher arrived at Beck's, Lilly's mouth fell open.

"Holy cow! This is awesome. It hardly looks like her house at all! Look at this." Lilly was struck by the decorations. But it wasn't the normal Halloween decorations. No silly lights and funny pumpkins. There were no animated silly werewolves or skeletons. There was nothing silly or funny at all. Beck had made a haunted house. There were webs that looked and felt real, the spiders she had put in were deep black with the red hour glass. As Lilly and Sher walked through the path to her front door, Sher enjoyed watching Lilly discover all the decoration Beck and girls had put together. The oak trees were hung with Spanish moss, with bats and cats as well. In the side yard was a cemetery that if Lilly didn't know better, would pass for a real one.

"She must have 40 head stones over there."

"She has 47, and counting. You want to go look?" Sher asked her

"Yes I do, this is so cool. She does this in a day?" Lilly asked.

"No she started yesterday, the girls came this morning and helped her finish. You've never been to one of these have you?"

"No, but I'm glad I'm here now. I really thought there'd be pumpkins and a few hanging ghosts and stuff like that. But this, this is so cool."

They walked around the fake cemetery and read some of the names on the stones. It was family. She had recreated the family cemetery. Right down to the pets they all had as kids.

"She even has the fish!" they both laughed.

They circled back to the front and finished the walk to the door. On the porch were several pumpkins. Only one carved. It was death. And he sat at the top of the mound of un-carved pumpkins. There was more moss and spider webs that covered almost every inch of the porch. A few candelabras were lit and soft music played. There were no screams, no fake lightning strikes and no witch laughter. But the atmosphere couldn't have been scarier.

When they opened the front door, the atmosphere was better. Candles by the hundreds lit the rooms. Cob webs dripped from the ceiling, the paintings on the wall's and pictures set throughout the house. Lilly felt as if she had stepped through time. Her daughters and nieces were dressed as pirates, wenches, and nobles. Her beautiful daughters were all dressed as pirates. Not the store bought Kmart kind. But the ruffed up and dirty kind. The outfits where perfect. Leather boots and linen shirts. Dark reds and deep blues.

All dressed as crew members. She could hear now, the faint sound of water. Like it was banging against a boat. She could also hear seagulls and faint shouts. As if outside there where ships with crew members setting sail.

"Isn't this great mom!" Sarah said.

"It is amazing. Do I hear ship talk?"

"Yeah, Aunt Becks got a CD a friend of hers made. It will take us right into a battle!"

"You girls look great, all of you"

Just then, Beck came down the stairs. Her costume was amazing. She had taken time to investigate what would have been worn in the sixteenth century for a female pirate. She was dressed in layers. Several dark red and cream color shirts. Brown pants with tall black boots. She was armed with replica guns and swords. Her hair was pulled lightly back and her face held scars she didn't have an hour ago.

"Ok, who are you?" Lilly asked

"I'm Lady Mary Killgrew." And she bowed to them. "Right now I'm commanding the *Maria*. But they, my traitorous crew, will turn me in to the Queen by nightfall, and Ill be hung from the neck til dead!"

'Beck, this place is awesome. I can't believe you go through all this, for Halloween."

"It's not just Halloween, It's my birthday too. And I love to play dress up. You two better get changed. The party starts in an hour. And I very seldom have late comers."

Sher and Lilly made their way up stairs to change and found Rory, Cybele, and Cleo in wench costumes.

"Wow! You guys look great!"

"And you two better hurry."

Sher and Lilly went to Beck's room and found it in shambles.

"Guess I know where everyone got changed. Good Lord, look at this room."

"Don't worry, Beck hires a cleaning crew for the day after her parties."

"You're kidding me. Must be nice. Well, I'm not here to clean. I'm here to relax and have fun."

Lilly pulled out her dress and laid it on the bed. Sher was dressing as a wench and with Beck as a pirate, her being a nobel seemed perfect. Though now, with the feeling she got from touching the dress, she wasn't so sure. But she wasn't going to let this dress stop her from having fun.

"It's not really the dress, Lil. It's the trunk." As if Sher could read her mind, she knew just what Lilly was thinking.

"Yeah, I know, but it still gives me the creeps."

When Lilly and Sher were done, they went back down stairs where some of Beck's friend were arriving already.

"This is a party that most of St Augustine wants to be invited to." Sher whispered to Lilly.

"You'll see why soon enough."

# *Eighteen*

Pirates, famous and crew, wenches and noble crowded Beck's house. Inside and out. Both back porch and side porches were full as well. She had hired a band to play, a local color called Those Guys. The best in St Augustine as far as the Osteen sisters thought. They all knew them, were friends with them and their families as well.

Lilly watched her girls get into the spirit of the evening. They were laughing and dancing. Something she hadn't seen them do in a long time. She found an empty chair on the back porch and tried to make herself comfortable. However the dress and all that came with it prevented her from being completely comfy.

She had mingled and met so many of Beck and Sher's friends tonight there was no way she would be able to remember them all. But she was having fun too. She even ran into a few high school friends, she hadn't seen since she married. She was sipping a drink when Sher came around the side of the house with a very good looking man.

"Hey Lil, you having fun?" She settled into the chair next to hers. She was lit up and glowing as she introduced Lilly to her friend.

"Lil, this is Gar, he works for the city, the nasty man." But she was laughing as she said it.

"Yes, I'm afraid that I do work for the city, and that's why your sister refuses to run away with me. Though I told her, tonight, I'm a terrible pirate who will have to kidnap her and force to her marry me." He was a nice man. Very pleasing to look at. The normal tall and broad shoulder that Sher always went for. His eyes were light blue and his hair was dark and curly. He held out his hand to Lilly and she took it to shake. He had a nice grip she thought. And then laughed at herself for sizing him up. Sher was old enough to run away and marry him. Or let herself be kidnapped for the night.

"Looks like every one is having a great time."

Lilly said to them.

"Yeah, so why are you out here alone?" Sher asked her. Before she could answer Sher looked to Gar and asked "can you get us a refill Gar, please?" She didn't wait for an answer. And he did try and give her one. He knew there were two questions there, can you get us a drink and leave us alone for a few minutes.

He took their glasses and went inside.

"I just needed a breather. All those people, trying to remember all their names, there's no way. But I am having a good time. Look, the girls are taking up the entire dance floor."

Sher looked to the side yard, where Beck had the band and dance floor. She grinned to see her girls and all her nieces dancing and singing. Most the young kids always went to the dance floor. A few times last year she caught some sneaking beer out. It was nice that her girls didn't feel the need to sneak beer. And it was even nicer when she saw Calista carrying back it inside.

They did let Cybele, Rory and Steph have a drink this year. But she saw that none of them really finished it.

"They always have fun this night. They don't miss not going trick or treating. Aunt Beck sets them up any way. She makes these huge baskets for each kid filled with candy and bath salts and make up and all sorts of stuff. They never seem to miss it. I'm really glad cuz this is the one night a year I get to do what I want with out anyone asking me questions. Think Gar might be what I want this year."

"You're a mess Sher." But she was laughing. She would never begrudge her sisters from one night of craziness. If sex was involved and no one got hurt from it, so be it.

Gar brought more than a drink, Beck was attached to his arm.

"Well, what a lucky man I am. To have the Osteen sisters all to myself. I'll be the envy of every man in St Augustine tonight."

"Yeah, go start some rumors Gar, I want to talk to my sisters for a minute."

"Oh well, it was fun while it lasted." He kissed each hand and bowed as he left.

"So why are my two very best sisters sitting out on the porch and not mingling?"

"Just taking in some air. And watching the girls dance." Beck turned to look. All the girls were there. Laughing. Having fun. She smiled and looked at Sher and Lilly.

"I swear they have more fun than some of the adults do."

They sat in silence for a few minutes. Watching and listening.

"My speakers out here seem loud, don't they?" Beck asked them

Lilly and Sher looked at her and shrugged. It didn't sound very loud to them.

While they talked about who they had introduced Lilly to, Sher thought she saw someone coming from the marsh.

"Who is that? And what the hell are they doing in the marsh at night?"

Both Lilly and Beck looked to where Sher pointed, but saw no one.

"I don't see anyone Sher, are you sure there's someone out there?"

"Yes, he's right there. Between those two trees. Almost at Beck's property line."

Neither women saw a man.

Sher stood up, and Lilly followed her. Lilly put her hand on her shoulder to calm her sister. As she did, Beck reached around and took Sher's hand, for the same reason. Before they realized what was happening, the world grew calm. Quiet. Black and white.

They took it all in. It only lasted for a few minutes. But they took in everything that they saw.

Five minutes later, they were back in their time at Beck's party. In color.

"What the hell just happened?" Sher whispered. She sat hard into a lounge chair. Lilly held onto the porch railing and Beck stood as if in a daze.

"We touched each other." Beck breathed.

"You and I were using out gifts and didn't realize it, then we touched. There's something going on tonight. Out there" she pointed to the march "we just got a glimpse of it."

"Holy shit, that's never happened before. We've never gone back into time."

"It's not over" Lilly said. Not so much to them, but just said it out loud.

"What do you mean?"

"If we touched again, I bet we could see more."

"It's never worked that way before, just touching. Something has to be going on first. And we don't usually all get to see what's happening."

"We will tonight." Lilly said as she turned to face them.

"What do you feel Lil? What's going on?"

"I don't know yet, there are a lot of feelings going on at one time. I can't separate them yet. But there's more coming. I know that. Keep alert tonight."

# Nineteen

Sher and Lilly never separated from each other again. Beck had to, she was the hostess. She wanted to make sure her friends had fun and stayed safe. She had a few of her guests mention the special effects of ghosts in the marsh and the sounds of cannon fire. Which she knew was not her doing. But took credit just the same. After an hour she made her way back to Sher and Lilly.

"Anything else?"

"Nothing more and the emotions seem to be weakening." Lilly told her.

"I haven't seen anything else. Just that one man in the marsh."

The three made their way to Beck's fake cemetery to find Cybele, Stephanie and Rory.

"What are you all doing out here. I thought you were dancing?" Sher made her way to her daughter and sat next to her on the ground. Beck did the same next to Rory. Lilly had to stand. She couldn't sit with the dress, and there were no chairs around.

"We were, but got creeped out by one of your guest's mom. I don't know his name, he just stared at us."

"No, Rory, you got creeped out, we never saw who you were looking at. We just came over for a break." Steph said to her mom.

Beck, Sher and Lilly looked at each other. With a silent "ease into this" look from all of them, Beck asked "What did he look like?"

"I don't really know, he never came closer then the Marsh edge. So I didn't get a close up. But he had to be a friend or something. He was dressed up and all. Who was he?"

"I don't know honey, I think you are seeing the same thing Aunt Sher is seeing to night. I want you to stay close to the other girls tonight. Still have fun, but stay away from the marsh." She reached for her daughter and gave her a reassuring hug and kiss.

"Mom, is something going on?" Cybele asked.

"We aren't sure, but if Rory and I are seeing the same thing, there's something going on. Don't say anything to the other girls. Just stay close to them. The parties almost over, what time is it Beck?"

"Its 11:34. Everyone usually leaves about midnight or one."

The three girls got up and went in search for the younger cousins and sisters.

"This is freaking me out a little. What ever is in the marsh tonight, it's strong. Or why would Rory see it too." Lilly asked

"Rory has been able to see things since she was little. All my girls can see, feel or hear. They have never shown much interest in honing their skills, but maybe I should have worked with them so that they can control it." As they walked around the back of the house, the man in the marsh made himself seen again. This time he was on her porch. He was leaning against the railing watching them come around. Only this time, they didn't realize he was their ghost.

# *Twenty*

Lilly saw him first. She noticed his sword and guns. They didn't look like the others she had seen tonight. His looked 'worn' somehow. The edge of his knives and sword were not sharp.

They stopped, before they came up the stairs. Beck and Sher realizing that he wasn't one of her guests.

"Now how is it you have all become friends? The pirate the wench and a beauty of a noble woman. Now I ask ya, how did it come to pass? Eh?" He crossed his arms and although his words were not threatening, they could feel the heat of his anger.

"Who are you?" Beck asked him.

"Aw now, you gonna claim to not know who I am, a game you want to play, fine, lets play a game. Hide and seek." He grabbed for Lilly's arm and pulled her to him. To their surprise, his hand made contact with her arm and she was pulled towards him.

"You hand over the coins, and she lives. You don't give me what I want Mary, she dies. And not in a nice way either."

Before they could reach Lilly, he was gone. She was left shaking and breathless.

"How is it he could grab me? Beck what is going on? How is this happening?"

"I don't know, Lilly. I don't know. Listen, sit here, Sher stay with her. I'm going to see everyone out. It's almost midnight, I'll tell them there's a family emergency, something and they have to leave. I'm sorry Lilly. Just hold on." She dashed away into the house. Sher could see her talking with some of her friends. They looked out the back windows to Sher and Lilly. As sympathy crossed their faces, Sher wondered what Beck had told them.

In ten minutes, everyone was gone and the girls were in the living room gathered around their mothers trying to make sense of what was happening.

"Ok, now wait. There's some ghost wandering around the mash tonight and it's trying to take mom hostage?" Steph asked.

"Looks that way." Beck said.

"Mom, is it the dress?" Sarah asked.

"I don't know, honey. Maybe I need to change."

"Reese, can you turn off the CD, I'm getting tired of listening to the cannon fire."

"Mom, it is off." Reese and Rowan said at the same time

Lilly, Beck and Sher stood up and walked to the windows. They saw nothing but Marsh and their reflections.

"Rory, turn off the lights. Turn off everything. Girls, blow out all the candles, lock the doors. And stay in a group. No one up stairs." As the girls ran off, Beck Sher and Lilly stayed by the windows.

"Beck, it's after midnight, its full moon and its October 31st." At first she didn't understand. Then it came to her. And the realization of the effects of the three things put together ran across her face.

"What." Lilly asked. "What does it mean?"

"Oh my God. And we are all in the same house." She put her hands to her face and rubbed her eyes.

"What Beck, I'm rusty here. What is it.?"

"It's October 31, Samhain. After midnight, where the veil between living and the dead is thin. It's full moon, an invitation for the dead to walk among us. I didn't think about this. I just thought how cool, a full moon for the party. And all of us, this house must be rocking tonight. The electricity between the three of us is always charged. But with the twelve of us, a god dammed coven. Plus that dress holding onto what ever it's holding. Shit. Shit!"

Just then all the girls came in.

Sher looked at them each in turn. They were old enough she thought. She glanced at Sher and then Lilly.

"What, I don't like that look at all Beck. What are you thinking?"

"Let's take it, let's take the ride and see where we go. If that dress has something to do with this tonight, let's do this. We have the girls for protection. We can sit in the middle and they will be here. Nothing will happen to us."

"My girls don't know anything about this stuff Beck. I'm not going to let them sit in a ritual circle and have something bad go on."

"There won't be anything bad, Lil. Our girls know what to do. They aren't going to let anything happen to us."

"No, I'm not going to do this Beck."

"Mom, do it. See what the dress is holding. Rory and Cybele can show us what to do. We will be ok."

Lilly looked at her girls. Sarah and Savannah looked eager to do this.

"Are you sure?" She asked each of them. And each said yes, with out hesitation.

"How long will it take?" Lilly asked Beck

"I have no idea. Rory, go get my bag." Rory went into the small office attached to the kitchen. When she came back, she was holding a large, what looked like doctors bag. The girls pushed the couches to the edge of the living room while Beck set up a temporary altar.

"Find a way to get comfortable Lilly, I don't know how long we will be. But you'll have to stay in the dress, we all should stay in what we have on."

The girls grabbed the cushions off the couches and placed them around the coffee table. Lilly took off her shoes and tried to sit, with help from Reese, she found a comfortable position. The girls would sit behind them in a second circle. As Beck started to cast her circle, Rory poured a second circle of salt. Before Beck started to call her quarters, she looked at Rory, Cybele and Stephanie.

"Keep everyone calm." She said.

And then she began:
"To the East, I invite the powers of Air
To blow out the old and bring in the new
on your winds of change
To the South, I invite the powers of Fire
To burn away regrets
and shine your gentle rays upon me for growth
To the West, I invite the powers of Water
To cleanse me of negativity
and purify my thoughts
To the North, I invite the powers of Earth
Let your renewing strength bury all ills
and open new paths before me"

As Beck called to the watchtowers, Lilly could hear Rory whisper to them as well. She had never seen a second circle cast before. But then Steve took her away from all this. And right now she really hated him for it. She might not be as afraid if she had still been allowed to practice her gift. Sher shook the thoughts of Steve and her anger away. She knew, even now, that you don't go into a ritual circle with anger and hate on your mind.

Beck finished by lighting the unity candle and reached for Sher and Lilly's hands.

"Before we touch, remember, nothing might happen or everything might. Rory, get ready, when we hold hands, you all hold hands and do not, do not let each other go until we are ok, you get it?" She looked sharply at Rory and Cybele. They knew what she meant, even if Lilly didn't.

"Wait, wait. Shouldn't we, I don't know, research this or something? I mean, we are just about to jump in here. And I think…"

"This, right now, is the best time Lilly. The moon, the day, us. I agree that it would be great to have some time. But we really don't. If we want to find out what's going on, its now."

Lilly stared at Beck and then Sher. She wanted to do this with them. She wanted to re-connect with them. But her girls were here. Did she really want them to be introduced to this so fast?

"Lilly, it's up to you. If you don't want to do it, we will stop."

She took a deep breath, "I'm in, let's do it. But hurry before I chicken out again."

Both Sher and Beck reached out their hands for Lilly. She took Beck's, and reached for Sher's. With a brief pause, she slipped her hand into Sher's and all went dark.

# Twenty One

When Aunt Lilly put her hand into her mom's hand, Cybele watched her mom and aunts disappear. At first she thought her eyes were playing tricks on her. In a way, they were. Her mom and aunts were still there, but they where shadows of themselves. Their eyes were open but they saw nothing.

"What's happened?" Steph asked.

"I don't know, I've never seen this happen before. They are there, but not there." Cybele answered.

"What do we do?" Sarah asked.

"We wait." Cleo said to them.

"How do we know if they are all right?" Sarah wondered out loud.

"I think we should be able to tell by the looks on their faces. What they see and feel should show up there."

"This is very creepy Cyb. Mom looks like she's in a trance or something."

"They are." Rory told them, "Mom and I did this once, she was learning to transgress. See who she was in a different lifetime. It was weird, but what she found out was cool. If this is anything like that, they could be out for 5 minutes or five hours."

"You're right." Came a deep voice from all around them. Steph started to jump up but Cyb and Rory both yelled for her to stay still.

"Who is that?"

"It's a trick, from the other side. If we break hold, mom and them are lost. DON'T LET GO! Steph, sit down."

"Very clever little girl."

"You're not going to scare us into dropping our mothers. SO you might as well go." Rory said.

"Who is it Rory?" Steph, Sarah and Savannah were on the brink of panic.

"I don't know, just be calm. Deep breaths and relax. Think of our moms. If we let go of each others hands, they are lost don't forget that."

"I'm not here to hurt them, I'm the one who sent them there." There was no place the voice came from, and yet it came from everywhere. They looked around the room. Trying to see something different. Cybele closed her eyes and tried to use her gift to lock onto the man. She knew he had to be here.

"You can't lock onto me Cybele. I'm here and I'm not. Again, I tell you I'm not here to hurt them. I'm here to make sure they find out what they need to know, to fix what went wrong that day."

"Who are you? If you're not here to hurt them, why not show yourself?" Cybele still tried to connect with him.

"I'm scared" Savannah and Sarah said.

"I am too" Stephanie admitted.

"Its ok, as long as we are inside this circle, no one can hurt us. They can play tricks on us, but they can't hurt us until we let go and walk out. But we aren't going to let go, right?" Rory continued to let them all know how important it was to hold on to each other.

Stephanie looked around the room ten minutes later. They hadn't heard from the man in that time.

"Is he gone?" She asked.

"I don't think so." Calista said. "I can still feel him here."

'Me too." Reese said. They both looked at Stephanie.

"Can you feel anything?"

"Like what?"

"Something kinda like heaviness, of the air around us hot and still?"

"Yeah, kinda like that. It kinda feels like something is sitting on my chest. Is that what that means? That's there's a ghost by me?" She asked, getting excited.

"Yeah, you can feel, like me and Calista and your mom. It's not just the feeling of ghosts, we can feel their emotions and stuff."

"This isn't the first time I've felt like this. It's happened a lot. I mean, really, a lot."

"We know, we noticed that when it starts, you get quiet and kinda draw into yourself." Calista said

"And you're face gets all red." Reese told her.

"Can we all do something?" Sarah asked.

"Yep. All of us." Rowan told her. Happy to be talking to them, to take their minds off of the man who still lingered around them.

"So, if you can feel his emotions, what are they? Does it feel bad?" Savannah was looking at her sister.

"It doesn't feel bad, it feels heavy. Just heavy."

"What can I do?" Sarah looked at Rory, then Rowan and Cybele.

"What do you think?" She asked her softly. Sarah was young, she didn't want to scare her. All that was happening right now would have been enough to throw the average person running from the house. Sarah was shy and quiet. But strong when she had to be.

"Sometimes I think there are people there that aren't there at all." She whispered. She was scared of what that meant. She didn't want to be a seer. She didn't know if she wanted to be anything at all. Right now, she wanted to be home, with both parents telling her this was a dream.

"That's because you are a seer, Sarah." They all grew very quiet. Just looking at each other. They could hear the wind outside. The marsh grass whistling it's tunes. They could hear their mothers breathing, slowly.

"Guess that means I can hear them." Savannah said.

"Yep, your one of us." Cybele winked at her. "Its you, me, and Rowan."

"OK," Stephanie said "So it's me, Calista and Reese. We can feel. Its Cybele, Rowan and Savannah that can hear and Sarah, Cleo and Rory that can see."

"That's right, and that's why we are here. With our moms, to help."

"Give me a little credit here." The voice again. They all jumped.

"God Damn it. What is it you want anyway?"

"Just what I said. I'm here to make sure your mothers come back safe and understand what they are doing. You might call me their spirit guide."

"If you're here to help, lets see you." Rory said.

"Yeah, I don't want to see him." Stephanie and Savannah both said.

"He can't hurt us."

While they were in the light of candles, they were able to see the back deck and marsh lands through the large windows. When they heard the rushing of the winds outside they all looked. At the edge of the deck was a small tornado of grasses and weeds. As fast as it started it stopped and in its place stood a man. Dressed in black and grays. He seemed very tall. His face was unshaven and hard. You could see the lines of age and hard living. He had his hands folded in front of him. His hair was jet black, almost purple. The girls all stared. Some too frightened to move. Others, to smart to move.

# Twenty Two

When Lilly slipped her hand into Sher's it felt as if she had been jerked off her chair. She and her sisters slammed down hard on the ground out side the house, close to the marsh. Standing up wondering what had happened, she felt a brief moment of panic thinking the girls were inside, alone.

They started to run to the house. Before they could get within 15 yards, it disappeared.

"What the fuck!" Beck and Sher said at once coming to a dead stop. In place of her house stood trees. She saw no other lights of any of the other houses that were close to her own. They saw, nothing. Trees and palms and wet land grasses.

"Where is my house? Where's my road? What happened to Lands End Drive? What is happening? I don't understand what just happened." Beck asked Lilly and Sher.

"You're asking me? Are you kidding? I have been back here for a month or so and you have dragged me back to this and you're asking me were your God Dammed house is?! Where are my kids!" Shock and terror were grabbing a hold of them. All of them.

"Wait, hold on. Listen." Sher said to them. They all stood still and quiet. In the distance they heard voices.

"I think they are coming from there." Sher pointed towards the north side of the marsh.

"Maybe we can ask what's happening." Lilly suggested

"I don't think that's a great idea. The last thing that was happening outside my back door was kind of pirate action. That could still be happening now." Beck answered.

"You're dressed for it." Lilly said with sarcasum.

"Yeah, and if you haven't noticed, you're not." They glared at each other.

"It's not going to do any good to be pissy with each other. We need to figure out what's going on. And maybe we can find our way home." Sher seemed to have her wits about her more then her sisters.

"They are getting closer, get down. Maybe we can figure something out by what they say. Be still. I really don't want to get caught in this outfit. Cuz I'm the wench, remember?"

They all squatted down and listened.

"He's gonna go ashore himself and get the girl. We are to wait and make sure no one sounds the alarm." One of the men said.

"What's he want with her any how. She won't be nothing but trouble."

"Don't let him hear you say that. He won her, he owns her now. He wants what he owns. You know the Captn'. He won't stop 'til he gets her."

"Where we going now? I thought we was to wait here?"

"I'm just gonna get a better look at what they doin'"

"You better not, he said stay here, we stay."

"He said make sure no one runs to sound the alarm. Who gonna do that from way back here. We are miles from town. No one knows we are coming. They think it's a ship full of flour. Not us." He laughed.

"Yer right, lets go have a look."

They slipped away into the night and Lilly, Beck and Sher sat up. Bewildered.

"Well, it seems St Augustine is being attacked by pirates."

They all sat for a few minutes trying to remember their history of the town they lived in.

"There were a few of them, right?" Beck asked, not really expecting an answer.

"Yeah, Drakes is the most popular. But there were maybe 3 more? I can't remember. Shit, now I wished I had paid more attention in history class." Beck and Sher kept coming back to Drakes raid.

"The only way to figure this out is to get to town."

"Wait. Even if we get to town, what are we gonna do, go up to a pirate and ask? 'Oh excuse me Mr. Pirate, would you be so kind as to tell us which pirate raid this is?'" Lilly was still mad at what was happening.

"Well, if you have a better idea, lets hear it."

"Yeah I do, I vote we sit down and wait."

"Wait for what? Rescue?"

"Listen you two, fighting isn't going to get us home faster. Beck, you did this once, right? Was the time the same? I mean is our time ticking by as fast as the girls? Or is it slower?" Sher asked Beck.

She thought for a minute.

"When Rory and I did it, I was under for about thirty minutes. She brought me back. But I don't remember thinking that time had gone by faster. It might have been a little different."

"Wait, Rory knows how to bring us back?" Lilly asked.

"Yeah, before we started, I talked with her. I told her that if anything happened like before, give us time to come back on our own, or bring us back after an hour."

"Ok, so again I say, let's sit and wait it out." Lilly sat herself down.

"Yeah well, here's a thought, what if when we left, someone else came in our place? Inside our circle." Lilly jumped up. She grabbed at Beck's arm. Fear on her face

"Can that happen? Did that happen?"

"I don't know. Really, I'm sorry Lil. I shouldn't have said that. I don't think so. I said it only to hurt you. I'm sorry. Let's just try and figure this out." Beck held onto her sister's hand. Lilly could see she was sorry.

"Me too, Beck. I'm just scared. I want to go home."

"We all do. So let's figure this out and get there." She said

They started walking through the marsh, oddly enough they started to relax. This was an area they knew. No matter what time frame they were in. They grew up in these marshes. And though there were new trees and different grasses, they were still their marshes.

"OK, so when we get to town, what then? I have lost the corset and the hoop for this dress. But I'm still in this dress and I'm still someone they might want."

"I don't think we should parade you through town. Staying on the side streets is our best option. I'm pretty sure we will be able to hear and see enough from there." Beck told them.

As they were walking they tried to fit St Augustine 2011 into this St Augustine they were in now.

"I think this is where the Cove should be. The boats should all be tied there." She pointed south of them.

"Which means" Lilly said. "We should go this way." And she turned north. There was a small area strong enough for them to walked across, but if one of them stepped wrong, the other two had to pull her out of the muck.

Again on hard ground, they walk for another twenty minutes.

"Don't you think we have been walking for well over an hour Beck? Do you think they are trying to bring us back and can't?"

"I don't know. We might be faster in time than they are. For all I know, ten minutes have gone by for them. I just don't know. And I don't have a watch to figure it out."

"Hey, guys, I think we are on May Street." Sher said to them

"Or where May Street should be."

"How can you tell" Lilly asked her as she looked around.

"Look at the way this area juts out." She pointed.

"I think you're right. Which means we should be getting close to San Marco Avenue. Right?"

"Yeah, but I don't know if its there yet. There might be a trail or something. But I doubt there's a road yet." And they began to walk in silence again. Beck stopped and turned around.

"Hold on a second." She told them. And she ran back to the water's edge. She began to wash her face.

"What are you doing?" The asked her.

"Well, if we are seen. We need to try and fit in. And all this make up on me is not going to work. I'm one of them. Or at least I look like it. But not with all this shit on my face." She stood up with a hand full of mud and smeared some on her face neck and hands.

"Oh, there's a look for you Beck." They laughed.

"Well, now I'll smell like them too. Let's go."

They turned around and began walking again. When they reached an area they thought should be close to where San Marco Ave would be, they turned south.

"Do you think the girls are ok?" Lilly asked them.

"Yes, I think they are fine. They are in my house and well protected. Rory and Cybele won't let anything happen to them, Lil. They will be fine." Beck took her by the hand and continued walking. After fifteen minutes, they started to hear shouts of alarm.

"Shit, we must be close." Sher said.

"What now, do we keep walking or wait here to see what happens?" Lilly asked them.

"If we wait, I don't think we are going to figure anything out. I think we should keep going. Quietly." Beck answered.

"I hate to say this, but I agree." Lilly squeezed Beck's hand that was still holding hers.

"I don't see anything familiar yet, do you Beck?" Sher asked her as they crept along.

"So far, no, and I still can't figure out the year. There's nothing here of the St Augustine that we know. No roads, no houses. Nothing yet. I think once we get closer to town, we might be able to figure some things out. Let's just be carful. I really don't want to get separated, or shot." They started again on their way.

"Shh" Beck held her finger to her lips and pulled them back into the bushes with her.

"What is it?" they asked.

"Look over there." She pointed to the east. "That looks like some kind of huts. I can see something or someone moving around."

"Oh my God" Lilly breathed. "We must be way back in time. Those are Indians Beck. We are looking at god damned Indians!"

"Shh, Lilly." Sher said and pulled her deeper into the brush.

"They don't seem to be in a panic though, do they?"

117

The three sisters watched for several more minutes.

"I don't think they have seen us. I think we should keep moving." Beck told them.

They eased out of the brush and slowly and quietly moved on.

"Ok, if that was one of the Indian towns they used to have here, then we have to be in the late sixteen hundreds or early seventeen hundred." Sher explained. "If I have my history right."

"Then we should be coming up on the town soon, but the shouting doesn't seem to sound any louder then before, why?" Lilly asked

"I don't know." Beck answered. "But let's keep moving."

Before they had gone too far, the Fort came into view.

"Hey, there's a corner of the fort, right?" Lilly said.

"I think so." Beck answered. "Do you see anything going on?"

"No, I don't see anything."

"Do you think it's done?"

"I don't know what was supposed to happen, so I don't know if anything is done or just starting or nothing is going to happen, or what." Beck said.

"Let's get closer and see." Beck said.

"Wait." Sher told them. "If we go that way it's to the fort, right, so if we stay along this path, its got to lead us to town. I think we should go to town first. If they are getting invaded, seems like all the fighting will be at the fort. To gain control of the town. If we go into town, then there won't be as many people to run into, and there won't be as much fighting, right?" Sher said to them.

"That's a good idea." Both Lilly and Beck agreed.

They stayed on the path and it did lead them to town. To a town they were not familiar with.

"Is that supposed to be St George Street?' Beck asked them. She turned to look at them and saw they were as lost as she was.

"Where is the cemetery?"

"I think it's too early for Huguenots. That didn't come 'til around the eighteen hundreds. Look there's no city gates either. It's just a street."

"Do you see any names? For the streets?" The three looked around. They slowly came closer to the town, but stayed well out of sight. In the distance they could hear the shouts and screams of the town's people.

"We need to go help them." Lilly said.

"No we don't." Beck caught her by the arm. "We can change nothing. Nothing Lilly. If we do, we don't know what we might go home to. One little change here and it could devastate our world. Our time. We can't do anything here."

"Then what's the point of being here? Why are we here if it's not to help in some way?" Lilly asked them.

"I don't know, but we can't chance it and do something that will mess up our time."

They came to a building at the end of the street. A house it looked like. Built of cypress and clay. A single story house. Other houses they saw were also single story. With a few windows and no glass. Small windows they noticed. The homes they saw were dark.

"No lights inside the houses." Lilly whispered. "Either there's no one home, or is hasn't started yet."

"I think these are all homes. I don't think this is a business section yet. Look at the fort. It's not the fort we know either. It looks like it's made of wood and coquina. Mostly wood." Beck pointed out.

Then they heard it. The sounds of guns and cannons. The thunderous boom of the cannons caught them off guard. Lilly screamed before Sher could get her hand over her mouth.

Men and women came rushing from their homes. Men were yelling at each other, asking what was happening. No one knew. Then a rider on horse back came plowing through the streets yelling of a pirate attack and for them to all seek shelter in the fort if they could make it. But they were on their own to get there. Women screamed for their children to come on. Husbands went back to the house to get guns and weapons.

Sher and Lilly stood and watched from the corner of the house. Lilly turned to ask Beck a question to find her crouched behind a barrel.

"What are you doing?" Lilly whispered.

"Look how I'm dressed? If they see me they will think I'm one of them and shoot me." Beck answered her. She stayed where she was. Lilly came around next to her and slid to the ground.

"I think waiting here is a good idea."

Sher continued to stand guard. She watched as the families from each home ran for the fort to take safety. She heard the sounds of hooves thundering close by, but never saw anyone. The town's people who didn't have a chance to get to safety tried to lock the pirates out. But she heard the screams of women and the laughter of the pirates. She knew what was happening. She looked to where Lilly and Beck hid. She knew Beck was right. If they intervened, something could go dreadfully wrong.

After ten minutes of standing, listening and watching her beloved town fall to its knees, Sher turned and sank next to her sisters.

"I hate this. Why are we here if it's not to help these people? What are we doing here Beck?"

"I don't know. But sitting here isn't going to answer that. I think I'll be safer going out there than you two" Beck started to say, but Lilly cut her off.

"I don't think so. You are dressed the part, sure, but none of those guns you're wearing work. I don't think we should break up. For one simple reason, we don't know why we are here. Until we know that, any one of us could get hurt, or killed. I don't know if we can die in this time. But I'm not willing to test that, are you?" She looked at both Sher and Beck.

"No, I'm not. I want to go home in one piece." Sher answered for both of them.

"So, what do we do?" Beck asked them.

"I think we need to sit this out. If we can gather as much information as we can, maybe we can go back to our time and research this assault. We have been able to see some of what the general public wears, at least to bed. The only thing we haven't seen are the pirates themselves. We also can see how the town is set up. If this is really St George Street, then we can see how the homes are built. And they are homes, not shops like we know St George Street to be. These houses are single story, built from mud, cedar and coquina. I don't yet see anything familiar. There's no city gate yet. The fort is built with wood and coquina here and there. But it's not the fort we know. Hughgnot Cemetery isn't even here yet. There are Indian villages on the north side and I bet the south side too. This is got to be just before the turn of the century. I bet we aren't in the seventeen hundreds yet." Lilly whispered. Both Sher and Beck listened to her knowing she made the most sense right now. All Sher wanted to do was go and help the villagers, and Beck wanted to knock some pirates heads together.

"Leave it to Lilly to be level headed now. OK, I agree with her. But I think we need to get a better look at the town. If we can get closer to the water, we might be able to figure out who is raiding."

The three crept out of their hiding spot and slowly made their way down the dirt street. Staying in shadows and along the houses, they managed to get to the other side of St. Augustine, close to the water.

"Holy Shit, I think this is Treasury Street." Sher said as they slid into it.

"Look, that's a supply ship." Beck said.

"Yeah, but that ain't supplies they're bringing. St. Augustine has been duped."

"Ok, so what attack do we know that fooled them into thinking they were getting supplies?"

"Are you kidding, do you think I know that off the top of my head. I have no clue." Sher said to her.

"You're the historian in the family Sher." Beck said to her impatiently.

"Yeah, *OUR* history, the Osteen history. Not St Augustine's history. I know half of us came from Norway and the other half, shit, I can't think right now. But I'm not a historian on St Augustine.'

"With all the shit you've found out you don't know anything about this raid?" Both women were losing it.

"Give me a break, Beck" and before she could finish both their heads came together with a hard knock.

They both turned to Lilly, looking at her as if she had lost her mind. She grinned.

"I've always wanted to do that. Now, if you two don't mind, shut it. We need to figure this out and fast. I don't want to still be here come morning. If we have to figure something out in order to get home, that's what we need to focus on. Not who does or does not know more about St Augustine's raids. So, let's shimmy up this street and get a better look, shall we?' Still grinning at the two of them, Lilly took the lead.

They made their way up the street avoiding crates and barrels that lined the street. When they reached the street end they glanced around the side of a building and saw the ship in full view.

"I can't tell if it's Spanish or English. Can either of you?' Beck said.

"Spanish, look at the flag." Lilly pointed.

"Ok, so it's a Spanish supply ship, that's good information. I don't really see any people any more though. Where in town are all the pirates? Sher said, glancing behind them.

"I wonder if the government house is built yet." Lilly said out loud, but more to herself.

"Why is it we can hear the shouts and the guns and cannons, but we aren't seeing the men behind them? It's almost like a ghost town, pardon the term ghost."

"I don't know, but the less we see of them, the better as far as I'm concerned." Beck told her.

As they turned to start back down the street, they heard several voices coming from inside the building. They fell behind crates and barrels for hiding. None of them moved, or hardly breathed.

"This way Governor, come quick." The three women saw shadows of two men coming down the street at a fast pace.

"We can get to the stockade from here." A man said. He was dressed in simple clothes, but the authority in his voice led them to believe he might be in charge of troops.

"Sergeant, what about the rest of the towns people?"

"We have gotten as many as we can so far, Sergeant Ponce de Leon has rescued about seventy men, women and child to the woods. On the other side of Indian town. They will be safe there for now. We must get to the stockade as fast as we can, there's no time to wait." They could see the sergeant was in a hurry, but the governor seemed to take his time.

"How many men are in the fort, right now?" he asked

"About thirty or so. We have few weapons, sir. But we can defend the stockade just the same."

"Ok, let's go, I hear nothing from the fort area as of yet. They will rob the government house first and they will make their way to it soon enough." With that, the men vanished around the building into the night. Neither of them seeing any of the three sisters that hid behind the crates.

The sisters stayed where they were for several minutes. Making sure the men were not followed.

"Ok, that answers the question of if the government house is there. And I vote on NOT going in that direction." Lilly said to them.

"Yeah, but we can't stay here either. If they are sneaking this way to the fort, then others will come this way too. Let's find another place to hide out." Beck started back to the end of the street. As they reached the end, they saw two figures across the alley from them.

"Shh, Isabelle" A man said." Please, hide in here, they won't find you in here. They are looking for guns and money. It's an old trunk. They won't even look in here." He pleaded with her.

"Jeremiah, I'm scared. I don't want to be separated from you. Can't we stay together?" She asked him, clinging to his arm.

"I need you to hide, if you come to the stockade with me, if they take it, they will take you. Please stay here and hide. I promise they won't find you. Just stay in here 'til I come back. I have to go, Isabella, please get in." She leaned up and kissed him hard. He put his arms around her and held on tightly to her.

"I love you" They could hear her whisper. "Please come get me soon."

She stepped into the trunk and knelt down as he closed the lid. He stood over it for a minute and said to her "I love you, you'll be safe, Ill be back soon." And with those words he dashed off into the night.

Lilly and Sher watched as he made his way down a side street that crossed theirs.

"Did you see what she had on?" Beck asked them, her eyes glued to the trunk.

"It's your dress Lilly."

# Twenty Three

"Who is he Rory?" Stephanie asked her in a whisper almost not heard.

"I'm known as Robert." He said to them. Though his mouth didn't move and the words echoed in their heads.

"As I have said, I mean you no harm."

"Ok, so what do you want? Why are you here?"

"Your mothers need my help. You are going to need my help as well. If you want to be able to bring them back." Again his mouth did not move. But each girl heard his words.

"You know, Robert, my mother didn't tell me about any spirit to guide her and my aunts home."

"I understand your hesitation, but within a matter of minutes, you will need to pull them back. If you aren't strong enough to do it, you will need my help."

"And what do I need to do to get that help from you?"

"Once you start to pull them back, if you can't, you need to open your circle to me, so I can join you to help."

Before he could finish what he was saying, the answer he got from all the girls was a firm no.

"There's no way we are opening this circle to you. In every ritual and circle my mother cast, one of the first things she taught us was to never allow someone in that you don't know. And you, being a spirit and all, are not coming into this circle."

"Rory," Stephanie began "Maybe we should listen to him. What if he is here to help?"

"Steph, I know that all this has got to be freaky for you. But trust me, we have been taught all our lives how to cast, what magic means, what to do and what not to do. And the first lesson we got was never, never, let anyone you don't trust into your circle. Once he is in our circle, he is in our lives. There's not an easy way to get him out."

"Your mothers are right. However, this time, you are going to need me to help, and if you don't let me in, I won't be able to help you."

"Well now for a spirit guide you sure don't know everything, do you?"

"Yes, Rory, If I cast my own circle around yours, I can help, but not with my full power."

"If we need the help, part of your power will be enough. And if it comes to that, we are still in our inner circle, you can't get to us."

They glared at each other for several minutes.

"You will need to start bringing them back in ten minutes. I'll be back then." And he was gone.

"I don't think he really is here to harm us Rory." Calista said. And Reese agreed.

"I don't feel any negativity from him. Actually, I feel nothing from him at all." Reese said to all of them.

"I know he seems harmless" Cybele said to them "But our moms have always told us not to pen this circle to anyone. A far as we know, he is a bad spirit that is powerful enough to cover his true intentions. I say we stick to what Mom asked, and get them back. What time is it?"

"It's almost time, about seven more minutes.'

"What if he shows back up?" Sarah asked

"So, he can't get in, so it's no big deal."

"Can he screw this up? I mean getting them back and all?"

"He can try to distract us, but we can still get to them. You three," She looked at Sarah, Stephanie and Savannah "need to concentrate hard. Do all you can not to look at him, or listen to anything he says once we start."

They quieted down for a minute, waiting out the five minutes left.

"How do we bring them back?" Stephanie asked.

"We call to them, silently, in our minds. Try and reach out to your mom, think about her, about her face, what she smells like. Everything that makes your mom, your mom. Once she feels your connection, she'll bring herself back, but you have to reach her first."

"What if we can't? We haven't ever done this before, what if we can't get to her?" Sarah and Savannah started freaking out. Shifting in their seats. And their faces were carved in fear.

"No worries, once we all connect with our moms, and they start to come back, we will all concentrate on aunt Lilly. She'll come back too."

"Make sure of it Rory. Make sure you can bring them back." He said. He was back, this time inside the house, next to the girls. Walking around them. Around their circle. Knowing that he couldn't get in.

"Listen, we don't need any help from you. If you're here to help, then go away and let us concentrate. Get ready every one, it's time. Steph, Sarah, Savannah. This won't happen fast. It can take up to thirty minutes. So don't panic if we don't get to them right away. Ok?"

She got nods from all of them.

"Ok, follow my lead. I'll talk out loud, but you talk in your head. ALONE." And she looked at the man circling them.

"Don't let me interrupt, Oh great witch." He sarcastically answered her. "I'm here when you need me."

But she paid him no attention. Her mother had taught her well. How to cut out any distraction that might be there when she practiced her gift. She was able to close her eyes without worry. She sighed deeply and began an easy chant for everyone to follow. At first she heard Lilly's girls, trying to keep up with her. Then one by one they fell silent. She reached out with her mind to each girl in the room. She could feel their concentration, their minds trying to cut out everything around them. Stephanie had the most trouble. Her mind kept going back to the man in the room with them. She thought to help her out, but also thought it would spook her more then she was if she heard Rory in her mind. She pulled back for Stephanie and went to Sarah, she was doing better but still had trouble cutting everything out, Savannah was doing the best out of the three. Softly Rory spoke.

"Just think of your moms. Just your mothers. Don't let anything outside of that thought distract you." Rory whispered to each of her sisters. In their minds they heard her say, "Help Sarah and Stephanie. Hold their hands a bit tighter. Let them know you're here." Her sisters knew she could invade their minds. Rory never did it maliciously. She always asked first. Never once did she invade them without consent.

## Twenty Four

"Are you sure?" Sher asked her

"Yeah, I'm sure. She must be the one we are supposed to find." The three looked at the closed trunk. Slowly they started to walk towards it.

"What are we gonna do? Open it and talk to her? I thought we weren't supposed to help anyone in this time?" Lilly asked both Sher and Beck.

"I don't know what we are going to do, maybe make sure nothing happens to that trunk?" Beck said to her. They stopped about thirty feet from the trunk.

"Someone's coming" Sher told them. They crouched down beside a building and waited.

Two men came from behind several barrels. Laughing a horrible laugh. They had seen her. They had watched her being put in the trunk for her safety. And now they were going to hurt her.

"What do we do Beck?" Beck looked at her sisters. Lilly's eyes were wet and Sher's were full of fright.

"We can't, we can't change this. I'm so sorry, but we can't." Beck turned away from what was going to happen.

"Ya think he'll let us have her when he's done?" One of the men said.

"Nah, he wants her for more 'in that." He answered his friend.

"Don't mean we can't have a bit of fun with her before we take her to him."

They reached the trunk and flung open the lid.

She screamed and tried to get out of the trunk. They boxed her in and held tightly on to her. One of them tried to kiss her. She used her hands to fight him off. When she slapped him, his friend grabbed both of her hands and held them down.

"Slap me will ya. I'll teach you who is boss!" His hand cracked the side of her face and she whimpered.

"Beck, I can't watch this. I mean, I can't just sit here and watch what they are going to do to her." Sher said. "I don't care about the rules of this time, I'm not going to let them hurt her."

Beck looked from Sher to Lilly while she could hear the woman crying and the men laughing.

She stood up and said to her sisters. "Stay here. Ill do the most that I can for her."

Taking a deep breath she walked out of the shadows and towards the men. She got ten feet from them and yelled.

"I wouldn't do that, if he wants her, he wants her unharmed." Was all she said. They stopped hurting her. They both turned to look at Beck, neither knowing what to do.

"Please, help me." The woman said. "My father can pay you, please. He has a lot of money. Just, if you can take me to him, I know he will pay you."

Beck said nothing, she didn't dare. Anymore help from her might alter the ending of this raid too much. She wanted to go back home to the home she knew. She just stood and watched as the men glared at her.

"We was just haven some fun. We wasn't gonna harm her none." One of the men grabbed her and pushed her back into the trunk. Beck could hear her yelling and crying to let her out. That her father would pay for her. What she didn't know was, her father was probably dead by now. Beck had gotten a good look at his face. She was the same woman they saw at Lilly's house. Only this version of her was innocent and beautiful. What they saw at Lilly's was an angry and hateful woman. What must have happened to her on that ship? It was more then Beck wanted to think of.

They hauled the trunk away. It was all she could do to just stand there and watch them take her away. But she did. As they walked away Beck could still hear the woman crying. The last thing she heard was her screaming for Jeremiah, saying he lied to her.

# Twenty Five

Their silent chanting had gone on for ten minute's so far. Rory and Cybele knew that sometimes it could take a while to connect with their mothers. But Lilly's girls were getting restless.

"I don't think its working Rory." Stephanie whispered. "Maybe he can help us."

"No Steph, you need to keep up the chant. And relax. I told you it can take some time. You can't think of anything else."

"Shh" Cybele said to them.

Rory looked at Stephanie, and thought, here goes nothing. She reached out to Stephanie and spoke to her in her head.

*Stephanie, its ok, it's just me*

Stephanie went ridged. She jumped and almost flung herself from the circle.

*WAIT! It's just me, calm down, it's me Rory, Stephanie.*

She didn't need to speak to Rory, Rory could see the question on her face.

*I have been able to do this for a long time. Now I need you to calm down. We aren't going to get our moms back without your help. And that means concentrating on the chant. If you lose it, your sisters will lose it too. And that puts your mom out there, with no one to bring her home, do you understand?*

Stephanie nodded her head and looked from sister to sister. They were both looking at her.

"It's alright, let's just keep it up." She smiled at both of them and closed her eyes. She thought, if Rory could talk to her in her mind, can she hear her thoughts too. When she opened one eye to look at Rory, Rory shook her head yes.

*I can hear you Steph.* Rory said to her.

*Is this really working? Or should we do something else?* Steph asked her

*If we don't get anything in five more minutes, we will try something else. But if they are very far in time, it will take some time getting them back.*

Stephanie relaxed again and fell into the chant with the others. Rory looked around for their unwanted guest and found him watching her.

He was on the other side of the back door. Standing on the back porch.

*That's pretty impressive* He said to her in her mind. *Not many people these days can do that*

She didn't answer him right away. She watched him watching her. She turned back to the circle to start her chanting again, but before she did she told him

*There's a lot about me that's impressive. And when mom gets back, she'll let me know if you deserve to see it or not.*

# Twenty Six

Beck walked back to her sisters. She felt defeated. She looked at Sher and then Lilly. She saw pity in their eyes. Not for her, but for the girl in that trunk.

"There was no more I could do for her."

"We know." She said and hugged her tightly. Beck sank down the side of the building and Sher and Lilly sat too. She rubbed her face hard with her hands. Biting the inside of her mouth so she wouldn't cry for what she knew would happen to the girl.

She began to say something and then quickly stopped. The air around them started to crack. She could feel the power in the air.

"Our times up." She said. The three sisters stood up. As if they had done this before, they were calm. Lilly closed her eyes and Sher rested her head on Beck's shoulder.

"Is this going to hurt?" Lilly asked, with her eyes still closed.

"No, it tingles some."

With one more glance around, they slipped their hands into each others. Once again, everything went dark.

## Twenty Seven

They landed with a thud, again, outside Beck's house. Between the marsh and her house. Beck sat up and shook her head to try and clear it.

Lilly and Sher did the same. They were still solemn. Their trip to the past turned on them in the end. What the girl in the trunk had gone through. To go from a sweet loving innocent girl to what they saw come out of the trunk. She couldn't imagine what she went through.

"Well, the first thing I want is a shot, then a bath and then about 24 hours of sleep."

"Good luck getting past the girls without telling them what happened." Sher said to Beck.

"Before we do anything, I think we need to write this all down. So we don't forget any of it." Lilly said as she helped Beck up. They tried to clean themselves off as they walked up the stairs. Beck held out her arms to stop Lilly and Sher. When they looked in the direction Beck was looking, they saw him.

"Who is that?" Lilly asked them both.

"I have no idea. But I think I have seen him before."

"I have too. Here, about the same time Lilly got grabbed."

"Well, let's see what he wants, before I throw him out." Beck marched into her house, with a big chip on her shoulder.

136

As soon as she touched the back door to open it, the girls felt her there. They started to jump up when Rory told them wait.

They were eager to get to their mothers. They wanted to hear what had happened and see if they were ok. Steph and Sarah and Savannah just wanted to touch Lilly to make sure she was really there.

Beck turned to the un-invited guest. Her eyes were ablaze. She was tired and mad. She just wanted her bath and a bed. Never mind the shot.

"Who are you and why are you here." Was all she said bracing herself for any magic he might throw her way.

"I'm Robert, I'm here to help." Was all he said. She waited for more, but he didn't give it.

"Help? What kind of help do we need from you?" She was on edge, she knew she was. She wasn't sure why she was being so nasty to him. She had no reason to think he was here for harm. But she still wouldn't let Rory break the circle. Not yet.

"Well, actually, I was going to help you back, but your daughters took care of that very well." He looked at the girls, and for the first time, he smiled. It was a nice smile. A calming smile. One without threat. Lilly and Sher seemed to relax a little. But Beck kept her guard up. She wasn't ready to trust him yet.

"OK, so the girls got us back, we are safe, why are you still here?"

He didn't answer right away. He looked from each sister, then to each daughter.

"You are a very powerful group. I thought that with what was going to happen to you tonight, that you would need my help getting back. But I was wrong. Your daughters did a fine job. You should be proud. Unfortunately, you are not done. There's still more to do in order to help Isabella out. And that is what I was hoping to get your help on."

"How do you know about Isabella?" Lilly asked him.

"I'm the one who sent you to the trunk. I'm the one who helped you to the past to see what had happened that night."

"You sent us there? How? Why? Why would you get me involved with that trunk?' Lilly was feeling used. She didn't like it. She felt as if she had been set up. And that was a feeling she hated, Steve used to do that to her. Trick her in order to get her to do something she knew she really didn't want to do. And now it was being done again, this time by a dead man.

"Before you get too upset, Lilly, I did not mean for it to be taken as a trick."

"Well, how else is it to be taken? You didn't come to us and ask us for help. You threw this at us and with out any explanation, you tossed us into the past. A dismal past. We had to watch what she went through. Knowing that there was nothing we could do." She was crying, before she knew it. She felt the hot tears slide down her face. She was standing behind her daughters. And she now understood why Beck wouldn't let them break the circle. This could be a bigger trick.

He said nothing. He looked from sister to sister. He could see mistrust had taken them. This is not what he had intended. He wanted their trust, he needed their help. He couldn't help anyone without them.

"I'm sorry, I will leave you to talk about this, I'll be back." And he was gone.

Lilly, Sher and Beck looked at each other. With unknowing looks. Was he really gone? They stood in silence. Looking around the room. Listening for any sign he was still there.

"Mom?" Stephanie said.

"I think he's gone." Beck said to no one, and everyone.

"Can we break the circle now?" Rory asked her mom.

"Yeah, I think we are alone. For now."

They all let go of hands. And Rory broke the circle. And there was a flurry of hugs and tears. Asking if each mom was ok. And telling about how scared they were. And how Robert was there the whole time their mothers were gone. Beck didn't like it. She didn't trust him. Lilly was with Beck. She didn't like being manipulated into helping. But Sher was quiet.

For an hour they answered their daughter's questions. Where did they go, what was it like? What year was it? What did St. Augustine look like?

Lilly and Beck told as much as they could. And then it came to talk about Isabella.

"So, she's the one in the trunk?" Sarah asked.

"Yeah, I think she is. And we know why she's angry."

"Id be mad too if my boyfriend locked me in a trunk!" Reese said.

"He didn't do it to hurt her. He thought he was saving her."

"What did he do when he came back and she was gone?"

"We don't know, we didn't see that. We left before he came back."

"Do you think you could go back, and help her this time?"

"No," Beck said." We aren't supposed to mess with the past."

"But Robert sent you there for a reason, right?" Rory said to her mom and aunts. "So maybe you can help out, just this one time?"

"I don't know that we are supposed to help her then, or now." Lilly said to her.

"If it was then, we failed her." Sher said. And the room got quiet. All of them thinking of what had happened to Isabella. Each thinking of how awful it had to have been.

"You know, it's been a long day, and a longer night. Let's put this away for now and get some sleep. I think we should all stay here, there's plenty of room." Beck said to them.

"That works for me, I don't think I have the energy to drive home anyway." Sher said.

When the house was quiet, and all were sleeping, he came back. He drifted from room to room, checking out each mother and daughter. These were his girls. He had watched over the Osteen women for centuries. They knew him, they just didn't remember him, yet. But they would, as they slept, they would start to remember.

# Twenty Eight

Beck, Rory Reese, and Rowan slept in the same room. As Sher, Cybele, Calista, and Cleo shared Rory's old room, and Lilly, Stephanie, Sarah and Savannah shared Reese's room. No one wanted to be alone. The comfort from family, sisters and mothers and daughters was needed. Each mother needed to feel their daughters. To know they were together and out of harm.

At four am Lilly woke with a start. She sat up and listened to the house. For several minutes she sat and listened. And then heard the foot steps in the hall. She slipped out of bed and crept to the door. As she held her ear to the door, she could hear the steps leading to the stairs. She silently opened her door a few inches and saw the back of someone going down the stairs. She thought at first it was Sher. She opened the door farther and slipped out of the room. Very gently she closed the door so it would not wake her girls. As she crept down the hall she could hear who ever it was in the kitchen. She stopped at the foot of the stairs and asked herself why she was sneaking around. She shook her head as if to clear it and went to the kitchen. Sher was there making coffee.

"You couldn't sleep either?' She asked without turning around to see who she was talking to.

"Actually, I was asleep, but your coming down woke me. Guess I wasn't as sound asleep as I thought I was." She sat across from Sher at the table. They waited for coffee without saying anything. It was an easy silence. Neither feeling as if they needed to fill the void with conversation. Before the coffee was finished, Beck made her way into the room.

"Yeah, me either. I have too much on my mind to sleep." She said to her sisters, before they could ask the question.

When coffee was poured and personalized, Beck gestured they go out to the porch.

"The sun rise will be fantastic this morning. I'd like to watch that before we dive into conversation.'

"Beck, it's four thirty in the morning. Sun rise isn't for a couple more hours yet." Sher said to her.

"Guess I need to make more coffee then." And smiled at her.

Lilly shook her head and smiled.

"That works." And she led the way.

They watched the sun rise across the marsh. They all sat quiet and content to just be with each other. With a few small conversations, they stuck with Beck's idea of waiting to see the sunrise before talking about more serious things. Half way through the wait, they added a small amount of Khalua to their coffee.

"I love this time of day. When the day is just beginning and the Gods start it out with such splender. Fills me with hope and promise. Like there's nothing I can't do."

The sky lit up with brilliant reds and oranges. Blues and purples joined in the dance as well. The sun was a large red fire ball that seemed to be dancing. They relaxed into the chairs. Their thoughts sinking into the morning sun rise. Listening as well to the birds that were waking up too.

As they watched the sun climbing higher into the sky, Robert watched them. He stayed the night out in the marsh. A place he had come to know as home. He had spent some of his time here, when he lived. But, most of his time spent here was after his death. His death was a horrible way to die, for anyone. He waited for them to start their conversation on what took place last night. Waited for just the right time. He knew it would come. He knew they would be full of questions, and not enough answers. They would, whether they wanted to or not, call to him. Either in anger or confusion. He drifted through the marsh and waited.

"Well, who is going to start?" Sher asked them.

"I don't know where to start. There are so many questions, not enough answers." Lilly answered her. They looked at each other, then at Beck.

"My first question," She said." Who is Robert, and why is he here?"

"Yeah well, he tried to answer that last night. But I don't think any of us were listening. Not really. We were too mad, and hurt and startled by him being here to listen to anything he had to say."

"Well, I doubt he has gone very far."

"I know he hasn't, he is in the marsh now." Sher said. "I see him, looks like he is waiting for an invitation to join us."

"Well, he can wait a little longer." Beck said to her. "I need to hash this out with you two first."

"So we still have more questions then answers." Sher said after an hour of talking. "This doesn't seem to be getting us anywhere. We keep circling around to the same things. What are we supposed to do now?"

As if on queue, Robert appeared at the bottom of the porch stairs.

"I don't think we said your name, and I'm pretty sure we didn't ask for your company, yet." Beck uttered.

"Beck," Lilly chastised her. "Give it a rest. We might just need the information he has to offer. At least listen to him."

"If you'd rather work this out without my help, I will leave you to it. But with the things I have heard, you are no closer to helping Isabella than you were an hour ago." His voice was courteous and gentle. Soothing.

"I'm sorry, I haven't had much sleep and I still don't like the way you were just there, in my house. Without invitation."

"Rebecca, I have had your 'invitation' on several occasions."

They stared at him, then turned to Beck. The look on her face told them she too had no idea what he was talking about.

"Who are you?" Lilly asked.

"You too, know me Lillianna, as do you Sheridan." His voice was musical. His face entrapped them. They all stared at him. Waiting for him to answer their question in more detail.

"I have always been here. With each of you. With the first Osteen woman with the magic. Her name was Sullann. She was from Norway in the year of 867." He let that sink in. Each sister blinked as if they were trying to take it in. What he was saying seemed impossible to them. When they looked back to him, he continued.

"She didn't know she was different. She didn't know no one else in her family, her village, couldn't do or see the things she could. She was a child. Just a child when her mother caught her talking to a man that was not there. They thought she was crazy. Simple. She was treated differently, but still loved. She grew to be very powerful. She married and had daughters of her own. Each held a different gift. Much like the three of you do." He stopped again, to reflect on the story he was telling them. How much to tell, how much to leave out, until the time was right.

"She was your wife?" Lilly asked him.

"Yes" he whispered, surprised she had guessed. "I'm here with you now, to help you. And in return, you will be helping me. I'm not asking you to do anything you don't want to do. But I need your help." They caught the need in his voice.

"Wait, you're our, what great grandfather twenty times or something?" Sher asked him.

"A bit more then that I'm afraid. I died in the year of 811. It would take days to explain it all to you, and we don't have that much time. But I promise Sheridan, one day I will tell you. I will give you your ancestry lesson." He smiled at her. And for the first time, she noticed how warm his smile was. How 'grandfather' like he was. His movement, his voice. He was her family.

"We will help you. Just tell us how." Sher said to him.

"Wait a minute, don't jump off that bridge yet." Beck stood up. Lilly reached out to take Beck's hand. She agreed with Sher and she wanted to show Beck what he was feeling. She knew as soon as she touched Beck, she would feel Robert's pain and honesty. She would know that what he was telling them was true. He needed their help. And they were going to give it.

"Ok, ok." She breathed. And sat. His pain was overwhelming. None of them knew why, they could see or feel that. But the new it was terrible. They knew it had to do with Sullann.

"What do you need from us?" Beck asked him.

He looked at each sister. He knew what each had to offer. And what they were capable of together.

"Do you remember Alton? The spirit you helped rest?"

"Yeah, at Joan's." Lilly said to him.

"That's the kind of help I need."

"You need us to get rid of a ghost for you?" Lilly questioned him.

"Can ghosts be haunted by other ghosts?" Sher said. Asking anyone who could answer.

"Yes and no." Robert replied. He was amused by their question. And their faces. "I'm not haunted by them, well I am in a way. I'm haunted in the sense that they are stuck here, in pain. And can't move on. I have helped them to move to the realm of Peace."

"The realm of Peace?" Lilly repeated.

"Yes, there are 5 different realms, you were always right Beck. There are different realms for different aspects of spirits. This, where you three are now, is the first realm, the realm of Life. The second realm, the realm of Death, is where spirits who are trapped unknowingly. People who have been killed by either murder or accident. They are there because they don't know that they have died. Once they figure that out, they "see the light' so to speak and move on to realm four. The realm of Peace. I'm here to help them cross over. To find the realm they belong in. To help them say good bye to the life they once had, and seek peace in what they are now. Sometimes it's very easy, now, with some like Isabella, its very hard." He grew quiet. They could tell he was lost in thought. Maybe a memory of her. He looked away, out to the marsh.

"I can see why you live here Beck. It's beautiful. Your eyes see things most do not. You see beauty in nothing." Again, he grew quiet.

"So you need us to help you cross Isabella over to, realm of Peace?" Sher said finally.

"Yes, and more. St Augustine is full of lost souls. They skipped the realm of Death, and are lost if the third realm. The realm of Vengeance. She is in that world. Reliving that day. The day you were taken back to. She is full of hate. So full of violence, contempt. I can't get to her. She blames Jeremiah. She thinks he left her there, on purpose. To be taken by the pirates. She was the governor's daughter. And he was a black smith's son. They were not supposed to be together that night. Or at all. She was considered above him. Her father kept telling her that Jeremiah only loved her for his money. That as soon as he could get his hands on money, from anywhere, he would dump her. But it wasn't true. He loved her. More than anything, he loved her. He thought he was truly hiding her. Her knew those men would want her, for her money, her body. So hiding her in that trunk, he thought was the best thing her could do for her. He had no idea he was being watched. But they found her, as you well know. And they took her to that ship. And what they did was horrible. I will never understand how man can do the things he does." He stopped, shook his head and ran his hands along his face. And if he was trying to erase the memory he had of her. "Well, there you have it, I need your help to reach her, to tell her that Jeremiah loved her, and waits for her forgiveness. Before he will cross to the realm of Peace."

"He's stuck too?" Sher said.

"He keeps himself stuck. Until she forgives him. He keeps himself in torment and agony over her. He refuses to cross. If he waits much longer, he won't be able to. He will be a shadow, and then he will be lost to me. And to you, with the power the three of you have, you won't be able to reach him once he becomes a shadow."

"What's a shadow?" they asked at the same time.

147

"It is a dark and dangerous thing to become. You can jump to any realm you want, but you won't know it. You won't remember that you were ever human. That you loved and were loved. That you have feelings of anything other then pain and regret. It will eat at your mind until it breaks. It's a dark place to be. I have seen it happen too many times. He doesn't deserve that. He deserves peace. She deserves peace."

"Ok, so, we will help. What do we do?" He smiled at them. He knew he would be able to count on them. Now to explain what it was he needed. And to let them know, this was to be the first of many.

# *Twenty Nine*

"So, are you thinking about Isabella or Sullann?" Beck asked Sher. Knowing she was thinking about Sullann. Sher was all into their ancestry. And not asking Robert, right away, about her must be killing her.

"I'm sure you can guess. I want to know so much, he knows us all. Right from the beginning. I have only been able to trace us to the early sixteen hundreds. And then I've lost some. But he knows us all. Can you imagine? Knowing so much, seeing year after year pass? All the changes he must have gone through. All the family he knows."

"Yeah, all the loved ones he has watched die. All the friends he has lost." Beck answered her.

Sher stopped, she looked at Beck. "Oh God, I never thought of it that way. How much love he has lost. Why is he still here? Why didn't he pass into, what realm of Peace?"

"I don't know. I'm sure we will know soon enough. I have a feeling, he is here to stay for a long time."

"So, when are we supposed to start this cross over thing?"

"He said he'd be back tonight, to get us ready. Where is Lilly?"

"She and the girls went for a walk. Through that old path down close to the marsh. I think she wants to talk to the girls in private. There's a lot going on that they aren't used to. They seem a bit spooked. Can't say as I blame them. I've been doing this for a long time, and I'm a bit spooked. Are we meeting Robert here or Lilly's house?"

"Here first, then her house later. I think my girls are a bit spooked by him to. The way he looks at you. Like he knows what you're thinking. He looks right down to your soul. Sizes you up, something like that."

"Think about it, he does know us. Right down to our souls. Who has known us longer? Not just us, but the Osteen's?" Sitting at the kitchen table, the two sisters sat silently for a while. Lost in their own thoughts. Of what the night would bring.

# *Thirty*

He glided around the marsh. A place he called home. Had called for centuries. Here he was comfortable. Here he stayed. He was called away from time to time. For a soul who couldn't find his or her way. A soul lost from the trauma of life now lost. He stayed in St Augustine as often as he could. Here were souls so long trapped, crossing to the Realm of Peace was almost impossible. Almost.

He had been thinking of the Osteen sisters for most of the day. Wondering how much he would have to tell them. And what he was going to leave out. He knew after sending Isabella and Jeremiah to the Realm of Peace, they would have a lot more questions for him. What would he do? Would he answer them, skate around them? Tell them a little to keep them happy or disappear until the next time he needed help. The last was not going to happen. There was no way he was going to leave them now. Now that they knew of him. They were his family. He was tired of watching them through windows and not being a part of their lives. He wouldn't intrude on them daily. They all had a need for privacy. Something that came to them naturally. Sullann had been the same way. There were times when he would lie to her and tell her he had to go. That he had to leave for several weeks on his ship. To sail away from her with his men to trade their ware's at the village north of them. It was a lie. She knew this as well. But he knew she needed her space away from him. And truth be told, he didn't mind the time with his men.

The last time he saw her was for this reason. He had been home for several weeks. She was growing restless for him to go so that she could have some time. Time with her daughters, time alone in the gardens. Time with her family. Her mother didn't like him. Never had. Her father warned him, often, that if he didn't do right by his only daughter, his death would be long and painful. Robert shook his head, his father in law was right. His death was painful. In ways Erik would never know.

They rode to the shore on horse back. One horse, two bodies. He loved riding with her this way. And so did she. She curled up on his lap and rested her head on his shoulder. His arms were wrapped around her in a tight hold. Though they needed the space from each other, they hated to leave each other. He dismounted the horse and helped her down. As they walked to the ship that would carry him away, the tears began to roll down her face.

"Don't Sullann, I'll be back before you know I'm gone." He kissed her forehead softly and ran his hands through her hair. She usually kept her hair in a long braid, but today she kept it loose. For him. He loved to run his hands through her hair and feel the silk between his hard calloused fingers. She leaned into him, and found his mouth. She kissed him with all the passion she had when she first met him. Their love was amazing to him. When she looked at him, it drove him crazy. When she touched him, in the simplest way, he felt all the love she had for him. In the tip of her fingers, she could tell him she hungered for him. She thought he was a good man. She would argue with anyone who said different about him. Her soul was kind and soft and loving. She trusted him. With everything that was in her. A good man, he thought now. A good man he said out loud, bitterly. He was anything but a good man.

To his village he was known as Ragmar, Sullann's husband. But he was known to the rest of the world as Ragmar the Dreaded.

# *Thirty One*

Sheridan paced the back porch. They were meeting with Robert again. He had left them to talk things over and think about what he was asking. For the past hour they had. Only for the past hour. That morning they thought they should meet and talk about it. They thought that an hour would be plenty of time. Because they all wanted to help. But now, again more questions.

"Sher, please sit, you're making me crazy with the pacing." Beck said to her.

"I can't help it, I want him to come now. I thought this morning, after he told us who he was and what he needed from us, I thought it was cool. But now, what are we taking on really?" She leaned against the railing. Looking at Beck and Lilly. But neither answered her. Neither knew the answer.

"I don't think its going to be that bad. We just did this for Joan. So why is this any different?" Lilly couldn't figure out why both Sher and Beck seemed so nervous.

"It's a little different Lilly." Beck knew that with Lilly being out of the magic world for so long, that she had forgotten a lot of the power that they held. Once this door was opened, once they slipped into this magic, there was no turning back. No matter how careful they were, something could slip past them and be unleashed.

"We did this already, we go in, we hold hands, we tell her that it wasn't supposed to be that way, that Jeremiah did not give her to those men, and she's ok."

"You don't think, with all this time, that Robert has tried something like that?" Sher said.

"You think, really, that all we have to do is talk to her and we, for some unknown reason, will be able to set her free, after all these years? Are you really that far gone from magic? Did you really let it go so much that you think this is going to be over in a matter of minute's? Shit. Lilly, if it was that easy, why is he asking us to do this for him?" Sher was standing again. This time right in front of Lilly. She couldn't believe that Lilly didn't see the dangers in this. That she had let her magic go for so long, that she really thought this would be over in a snap.

"Wait a minute. Yeah I've let it go. And yes it's my fault. But I'm not stupid Sher, so don't talk to me as if I'm an idiot. If there's something going on here that you two would like to share with me, I'm all ears. Because as far as I know, this isn't much different than what we did for Alton. You're right, I've been out of it. And I'm sorry." She had to take a breath. She knew her temper was about to explode. Her life for the past few months had come undone. And Sher yelling at her wasn't helping.

"Sher, just relax for a minute. We are all running on empty today. We haven't had much sleep in the past few days. So let's just take this one step at a time." Beck was standing between her sisters. There was no way she could let this fight start now. Lilly was holding in a lot of pent up anger. Anger she figured started about fifteen years ago.

"Let's wait and see what Robert tells us."

Lilly cooled herself and Sher backed off. Both of them knowing it wasn't each other that they were mad at. It was the unknown.

Sher walked back to the edge of the porch. And Lilly laid back on the chair. Beck went inside and a few minutes came back out with three shots of tequila. She handed a shot to each of her sisters and said "I know this isn't our usual drink, but I think it's a perfect choice for tonight." She held up her arm and each sister did the same.

"Cheers" they said. Lilly held out her hand to Sher and she willingly took it.

"Sorry I snapped." Sher whispered to her.

"Me too."

"I'm glad to see the fire is out." Robert said to them as he approached the porch. He leaned on the railing and looked at each in turn. He knew he was the start of the fight. Not the result. He also knew if they fought now, before they had a chance to help Isabella, there would be no helping her. Their anger would feed hers. He had to keep them calm.

"Yeah, well, we all have short fuses right now. So start talking and let us know what we are doing tonight."

"If your anger for each other doesn't subside, you won't be able to help her. She will feel that first, and she will feed off that until she brings you three to your knees." He calmly said.

"Well, don't sugar coat it for us. Shit Robert. Can you maybe ease us into this, just a little?" It really wasn't a question. Beck was starting to get angry now herself. Bastard, she thought. Give us a break.

He lowered his head. He needs to be careful with her. They were time bombs, all three of them, ready to go off.

"I'm sorry ladies. If you'll let me try again, I will try and watch how I say this to you." He bowed, not in a mocking way, but as a sincere gesture.

"Lilly, this is not going to be as easy as it was with Alton. I'm sorry to say that. I have for years been trying to get to Isabella. She refuses to listen to anything I have to say. At first it was because I am male. But after years of just listening to her, she began to trust me, a little. There have been several times that I have almost gotten over the anger she holds, only to have her push me out leaving her to feed on her anger and hate. The longer she stays, in that trunk, feeding, the harder she makes it for me to get to her. I haven't been able to get near in fifteen years. By close, I mean able to talk to her. When she feels me coming, she hides in the realm and I can't find her." He made his way up the stairs and closer to them. They could feel the chill that he brought with him. This time, it chilled them to the bone.

"I don't know what we can do. If you have been trying for years to get to her, how are we going to get to her tonight?" Beck asked him.

"Tonight is like a trial run. To see how close you are able to get. She might listen to some of what it is you are trying to tell her. She might sense that I am close and cut you out right off."

Do you think that we should try and get to Jeremiah first? And maybe get him to come close to her?" Sher asked.

"I tried that, he won't come too close because her anger sears him. Cuts him. Her hate for him only intensifies his guilt."

"Ok, so we go to Lilly's house and what, just open the trunk and start talking?"

"Yes, and no. You can't open that trunk first. Not until you've cast your circle, with her on the inside. Your power is the three of you. When you touch each other. That power is stronger, I think, than hers is."

157

"You think?" Beck caught that right away. "You think? You mean you aren't sure? If her power is stronger then ours, Robert, she could hurt us, right?'

"Yes" was all he said. He looked down into the night marsh. He waited.

It sank in to all three women. They sat quietly thinking of the dangers that faced them if they went along with him. Each sister looked at the other in turn.

"Well, are we voting, or what?" Sher asked them.

Lilly took a deep breath and let it out slowly. She didn't want to do this. But she knew she would. She knew what being trapped felt like. She knew sorrow and pain. She knew she would help. Even if Isabella was a ghost. She was someone's daughter once. Someone's lover and friend. She was in. All the way, and she said as much.

"I'm in, I'm in until we can release her." She looked at Robert, then Beck and Sher.

"Same here." Beck said. She reached for Lilly. Knowing how much harder this would be on her.

"Well, I guess in for a penny, in for a pound." Was Sher's answer. "So what next?"

"Meet me at Lilly's house" and he was gone.

# *Thirty Two*

As they drove into the drive way, they felt an uneasy cold settle upon them. Sher turned off the SUV and they sat there. Waiting. For what, they weren't sure.

After a few minutes of silence, Sher asked them if they had changed their minds.

"No," Beck said to her." I'm just getting my nerve up. Sure wish I had had a shot of something before we left the house."

Lilly grinned at her.

"You didn't, did you?" She asked.

"I did." Lilly opened her purse and pulled out a bottle of tequila. Beck grinned at her then Sher.

"Well, a shot for courage?" Lilly asked, knowing the answer.

"Me first." She took the bottle from her. The liquid felt cool at first. A few seconds later came the burn. The wonderful burn that warmed her ears.

"That's nice." She murmured.

They all took a drink and felt the welcome burn down their throats.

"Liquid courage." Their mother used to say.

"Mom used to take a shot before she did anything risky." Beck told them.

"She did?" Lilly asked surprise. "I don't remember her drinking anything but beer."

"I remember, her and gran." Sher said. She was looking at the house when she spoke to her sisters.

"I really don't know what we are going to find in there." She turned to face her sisters.

She wanted one of them to tell her it was going to be ok. That they would walk out of that house the same way they walked in. Lilly would tell her that, but she wanted to hear it from Beck. Beck would know for sure. If she couldn't say it, then there was a good chance that it wasn't true.

"Beck," Lilly stated.

"I don't know. I truly don't know. But, we said we would help. So, let's go help."

"Wait a minute." Lilly held her shoulder before she could go any farther. "If it gets bad, so bad that there's a chance we could get hurt, very hurt, we stop. I say we stop. I feel for her, and I'm sorry she's stuck there, but she's not worth one of us getting hurt. And you know what I mean about hurt. Not just a scratch, but really hurt or maimed or" she couldn't say it. She swallowed hard. The tears started to build in her eyes. But she shook her head to clear her eyes, and her mind.

She and Sher followed Beck out of the SUV and into the house.

As soon as they crossed the threshold of the back door, they could feel the hate that had been building since Lilly brought the trunk home.

"Didn't the girls come here the other day and get a change of clothes?" Sher asked.

"Holy shit, how did they not feel this?" Beck said.

"It feels like someone's sitting on my chest."

160

"Did you leave the heater on Lilly? It must be over ninety degrees in here."

"There isn't any real heat. There's a small furnace by the shop. But that's not going to make this kind of heat."

They stood in the kitchen. Looking through the door way and into the living area. They could almost see the heat ripples in the air.

"Are you ready" His voice came from behind them. All three jumped.

"God damn it!" Sher whispered.

"You almost got your head knocked off." Beck said to him before she remembered that would be impossible.

He looked at them with a smirk.

"Jumpy are you?" He asked all three.

"Well, I don't know, what do you think?" Was Beck smart answer.

"Well, standing here is not going to get her moving on, is it?" Was his smart answer.

As they entered the front parlor, the temperature dropped to ice.

"Ok, that sucks, I'd rather be stuck in the heated rooms." Lilly said.

"Ok, so now what?"

"Move the trunk to the middle of the room, and cast your circle around it."

"Around it? Are you kidding?"

"No, Rebecca, I'm not kidding. You must contain her. If you cast the circle without her in it, you will unleash her. You must contain her." Robert told her. He looked at them. Could they do this he wondered? Could they really do this? Maybe he was wrong. Maybe he should just tell them to go. And he would try again, alone.

"Ok, let's cast shall we." They were nervous. All of them. Beck usually was the one who ran into things like this head first. But not tonight. Tonight she walked with caution. Tonight she would think about everything she said and did, before she said and did it.

They pulled the trunk to the center of the room and moved all the other furniture to the outer walls. There was more than enough room for them to cast with comfort. And a clear space to get out of the room fast if they needed to.

"Lillianna, you must cast this circle, and you must to it completely." He said in a whispered voice.

"Robert, I haven't cast a circle in years. I don't know if I remember how." She turned to look at him. Her face was etched in fear.

"Can we help her?" Beck asked.

"Yes, simple help. But this is her house and she was given the trunk that binds Isabella. She must be the leader. In all that is done tonight, she must lead." He wanted to touch her, to comfort her in some way. But he could not. Her sisters walked to her and reassured her that she was strong enough for this. She could do this. And if she faltered, they would be there to help her. He smiled at them. They were each others greatest strength as well as hardest critics.

"Robert, can I read from Beck's book as I cast?"

"Yes, yes, you can." That calmed her some. Beck and Sher came into the area that would be on the inside of their circle. Beck pulled out her book and handed it to Lilly. She also pulled out the candles they would use and other items for a full cast circle. She handed Lilly the black salt and moon water. She arranged a semi altar by the trunk on a small table Sher had moved from one of the girl's bedrooms. She laid a black cloth across it and set out three candles. Then she pulled out the myrrh incense and set it on the table too.

"I brought everything." She nervously said. "I didn't know what not to bring." She looked at Robert. Wondering if she brought the right things.

"We will use it all." He said to her and smiled. For some reason, she felt like a child, wanting her grandfather's approval. She shook that thought away. She had never known either of her grandfathers. And not once, until just now, had she given them much thought.

"Who was he?' She asked Robert. He knew. He knew what she was asking.

"He was a good man who couldn't take the magic." She wanted to ask more. Was he still alive? Was he still in St Augustine? Did he know who they were? But it wasn't the time for it. Someday it would be. But not right now. She looked away. Back to the altar.

Lilly and Sher joined her.

"Ok, start east and pour the salt as you call the quarters. Once you do that, you can take a minute to begin the candles. But as you call and pour you need to be ready. You need a rhythm. Don't stutter or falter. If you don't get a good solid line of salt, if you some how have a break in it, anything can get it." She and Lilly looked at each other, then at Robert.

"Well, other than this very mad lady in the bad trunk."

"Ok, ok." Lilly said. She closed her eyes and took a deep breath. She let it out slowly and took another. "Ok, I think I'm ready. She turned east and held out her hand that had the bag of black salt in it. She looked once more at Sher and Beck, and then she began.

"Guardian of the east, powers of air, you who are our thoughts and the wind upon our faces. The winged eagles of the skies who are the morning breeze and the wrath of storms, we call upon you and invite you to witness this rite."

She poured the salt and read the words in a graceful motion that even surprised Robert. Her hands were shaking, but her grace was fluid. She took another deep breath and began again.

"Guardian of the south, powers of fire, you who are our passions and the hearth. Great snake that lives within the coals of our home fires as well as the wild fires. I call upon you and invite you to witness this rite." Again she breathed.

"Guardians of the west, powers of water, you who are our emotions and pure love. Gentle Wales of the waves, who are the morning dew and the torrential rains. I call upon you and invite you to witness this rite." Again she breathed. Her hands shaking so badly she didn't think she would be able to read Beck's hand writing. She could feel the evil within the trunk. She knew what was going to come when they opened it. If Isabella gave them the chance to open it. If she didn't burst through on her own. Again she breathed, and one more time she called to the quarters.

"Guardians of the north, powers of the earth, you who are the stabilizer and nurturer. Powerful as the Buffalo who stands solids as the mountains, I call upon you and invite you to witness this rite."

She finished pouring the salt, and turned once more to the east.

Lilly walked to Sher and Beck and took the matches from Sher and knelt at the make shift altar they had set on the small table. As the match lit the middle candle, the room darkened. Lilly hesitated.

"Keep going Lilly." Robert told her.

"I can feel her coming." Lilly said without looking up from the candles.

"I know, I can feel her too." Sher whispered.

She struck another match and lit the Goddess candle on her right.

"I call upon the Goddess, creator of women. I welcome you to empower this magical circle." She touched the match to the candle on her left, the Gods candle. "I call upon the Gods, creator of man. I welcome you to empower this magical circle." Before any of them had time to breathe, the trunk exploded and Isabella was in the center of their circle.

# Thirty Three

The three of them jumped. They sat frozen in place as they watched Isabella take form. Her body swirled left and right as it tried to solidify. Her face twisted in hate and malevolence. Her eyes sharpened first. What they saw for the few moments, as it took her body time to catch up, would be unforgettable to them all. Her eyes, so full of hate.

It was more then hate. It was more then anger. Her eyes were the window to her pain, to her full emotions. The misery and torment she was enduring. Year after year had built itself into something so chilling, they didn't know if they would be able to reach her. Sher looked over at Robert.

"Don't look at him" a treacherous voice called. "You have opened this trunk yourselves, now you will deal with what follows." Her voice came from nowhere and everywhere. The hairs all over her stood up. She grabbed for Lilly and Beck's hands. They gave them. She could feel the power in the room. Theirs and Isabella's fighting. The good and the damned trying to take control.

Her body solid and her eyes now concealed. She looked at each sister in turn. As if she was measuring them to see who was the weakest. She chose Lilly.

"You think you can do something different than Ragmar has?" None of the women knew who she spoke of. With a wave of her arm, she indicated to the man they knew as Robert. "His former life."

Lilly decided to try and talk. Her voice but a whisper.

"Isabella, the day you died, it was a mistake. Jeremiah…"

"DON'T speak his name to me! He stuck me in that trunk knowing what was coming for me! He never cared, just like they said. He was only after my father's money. As soon as I spoke of marriage to him, he bolted for something better and left me to die in the hands of those men." The air twisted, became thick. Sher felt as if a weight was pressing down upon her. Beck couldn't find the strength to speak, much less breathe.

"Please, hear us out." Lilly seemed to be the only one of the three who could still think straight.

"Why, so you can lie to me as he has," again she waved her arm to Robert. "He has come to me time and again speaking of how Jeremiah loved me and has locked himself in a place of torture as I have. But I don't see him, do you?" her fury swirled around her. One minute there was a cold revulsion that filled the room, the next it was replaced by the searing torment of a broken heart.

"He is stuck in this realm, Isabella. I can show you." She turned to Robert.

"Can I show her?"

"No, not when she is like this, he will not come."

"So, he is afraid to show his face to me. After what he has done, he should be. I will not forgive him. That is what you have come to ask me. I know this. But I will not ever. I live this, every day I relive what happened to me. What he helped happen to me." There was a moment of weakness. She was not as angry right now. Lilly could feel it slipping. The hatred giving way to heartache and confusion.

"Isabella, we saw some of what happened to you that night." She had a little time here. She knew it, she had to make the most of this of this brief change.

"He thought he was saving you. He thought by putting you in the trunk he was hiding you from them." She tried to get out as much as she could. She saw the doubt in Isabella's eyes. She thought she was getting through to her.

"His torment is as strong as yours. Only its pain and sorrow." Wrong thing to say.

"NO! I will not listen to your lies. He is caught in the world he created by his guilt. Not his sorrow." Lilly could see the hatred twisting up and down her spine. She could feel the room begin to change. Before any of them cold react, Isabella was gone. But not before her power had knocked them backwards. With their breath knocked out of them, they scrambled up to see what had happened. Their candles were blown out and the protective circle of black salt blown away.

They sat up and looked at Robert. In his face they saw years of pain. Years of failure.

"I'm sorry Robert." Sher said to him.

He looked at her.

"You did well." He said. They were confused. Looking at each other then back to him.

"We failed." Lilly said.

"No, she had a moment of doubt. You did not fail. You planted a thought, she doubts her anger now. You need to cast you circle again."

"Now?"

"Yes, bring her back before she can rebuild that hate for him. Bring her back and tell her again, the same things you have said. Lilly, you know the pain she feels. Use your pain to reach her."

Lilly reached for the bag of salt and began to call the quarters again. Sher and Beck sat and waited. After the candles were lit, Lilly called for Isabella again. And again she came with a powerful hate. Only this time, her form was not as dark and loathing as it was before. This time, there was little light in her face.

"Why do you do this to me? Why won't you let me be? Is it not bad enough that I must relive this memory every day, but you have come to show me more?" Her voice was hateful, but it was also full of sorrow.

"I'm sorry Isabella. We are trying to help you. I see your pain. I know your pain. You think the man you loved so much betrayed you. I know that kind of pain. My husband did."

"Then why do you make me relive this? Why are you forcing me to forgive him?" Her face swirled with confusion.

"Because he didn't do what you think he did. Again, I was there I saw what he did…"

"Then you know! You know he stuffed me in that trunk for those men to find."

"'No, not for those men to find, for him to find when the raid was over." Lilly came closer to her. Was she like Robert? She wondered. Could she touch her? The closer she got, the colder it got.

"You don't know what I went through" Her eyes caught Lilly. The blackness of them scared her. The evil twisting of her face made Lilly take a step back. But it was too late. Isabella had reached out and grabbed Lilly's arm. In that second, Lilly was taken back to the night Isabella was taken aboard the ship.

# Thirty Four

Lilly was confused by the darkness, the tightness that she felt. She couldn't move her legs. She was trapped in something. Where was she? How did she get here? She was just standing in her home, with her sisters. Wasn't she? Her mind felt thick. She could hear talking, laughing. What was going on? Did she faint?

"Sher? Beck?" She yelled.

"Shut up in there!" Someone yelled.

And then she knew. She was in that trunk a hundred years ago.

"Isabella! Let me out of here!" She yelled. Again she heard the men who carried her. They shook the trunk, and then dropped it. She hit the ground hard and cried out.

"Now you'll know, now you'll know." She heard Isabella whisper.

"No, please Isabella, please. I know it was horrifying for you. We aren't trying to take that away from you. Please let me out, please." She started to cry.

"We will let you out as soon as we get to the ship! He'll be wanting to see you then!" And they laughed. A horrible chilling laugh. She heard nothing from Isabella.

When they boarded the ship they dropped the trunk. Again she cried out. She could feel the ship rolling with the water.

They kicked the trunk across the ship and down some stairs. She heard a door open and again she was picked up and dropped a few feet away.

The voices she heard were muffled. She listened as foot steps came closer to her. And then the lid of the trunk opened. Her eyes needed time to adjust to the light. But she could make out three men in front of her as she stood up. Looking down she realized, this body was not hers. She looked like Isabella. Dress and all.

"Your father is the governor?"

"Yes" She barely spoke. This was not a pirate she thought of. In the books she had read, this was nothing like them. They were romanticized in those books. There was nothing kind about the man that stood in front of her. There was nothing warm in him. He was cold. Callous. Indifferent to the fact she was also human. But not that she was female.

"If I do not get what I want from your city, I will hand you over to my crew. And what they do with you, I do not care. So for your sake, I hope they give me all St. Augustine has to offer." That was all he said to her. She was then stuffed back into the trunk and shoved to the side of the room.

She spent hours in that trunk. She could hear men coming and going. She could hear them talking but could make out what they were saying. Then she heard them come close to her, and the lid once more opened. They pulled her out with hurtful hands. When she tried to shield her eyes from the lights they held her arms to her side.

"Well, your fair city gave me what I asked for. But, I'm not feeling very friendly. So the deal is off. You won't be going back to your father."

She stared at him. Not knowing what to say. If she heard him.

"But, but you made a deal. You said if they gave you what you wanted, you'd let me go."

She heard the words she said. But she felt as if someone else was saying them. And of course, someone else was.

"Yes, I did, but I lied." That was all he said. The men that held her pulled her from the room. She could hear them dragging the trunk as well. She couldn't fight them. She had been locked in the trunk for so long her arms and legs barley worked. The door slammed behind her. And those two men that held her laughed.

"Don't worry, it will be over before you know it." His breath smelled rotten. When he smiled his teeth were stained brown and green.

They took her up a flight of stairs that opened to the outside. The sea breeze skimmed her face and felt warm. The sun was blazing and seagulls flew over head.

"Enjoy these next few minutes, love, it's the last time you'll see day light." This time all the men on top roared with laughter. She scanned the crew. Old and young alike looked at her as if she were a last meal. Fear gripped her. She tried to stop them from taking her back down a different set of stairs. Stairs that were leading her to her undoing. To her death.

Once they got down stairs to an alley way, they steered her to a small room, like a closet. There was a single mat on the floor where they threw her. One of the men straddled her and grabbed her wrists. The other man gave him some rope to tie her. He wrapped the rope around her wrists and pulled them above her head. With her arms bent he tied the rope behind her.

"Well now, I'd say you were good and tied. I don't think your gonna put up much of a fight now are ya?"

"Give her a try, see how she fairs. You have the first shot at the new lady, I'm next before they all get down here and there's nothing left of her."

It began. She felt everything. The dress being ripped away from her. The pain in her arms when she tried to fight him off. The bone crushing weight he had on top of her. The ripping inside her as he thrust inside her unwilling body. She felt the burning tears as they rolled down her face.

"And this is just the beginning." She heard Isabella whisper in her ear.

"Why, why, please stop this." Lilly cried.

"I'll stop soon enough." He said to Lilly. Thinking it was him she was talking to. But it was Isabella she was pleading with.

She was raped for days. Given just enough food and water to keep her alive. But not enough to give her any strength. She fought for hours. But then gave into them. Some slapped at her. Some beat her. Some kicked and spit on her. But they all laughed in the end.

She didn't know how long she had been there. Trapped in that room. She had no clothes anymore. Her hair was mangled with spit and dried blood. Her body covered in bruises and cuts. Some ribs had been broken. She could feel no pain anymore. She could feel nothing. When they came and untied her, and stuffed her back into the trunk, she was grateful. She felt them carry her up some stairs and she thought she might get to see the sun. She thought for a moment they were taking her back home. That the captain had had a change of heart and was taking her back to her father.

They stopped and lifted the trunk higher, with a few swings she felt like she was flying. She hit the water with a great splash. With cold fear mixed with fury, she knew what had just happened. They threw her off the ship. She was in the ocean, locked inside this trunk. This trunk that Jeremiah put her into.

Her last thoughts were of Jeremiah. Not the men who kidnapped her. Not the captain who lied to her. Not the men who raped her. But of Jeremiah. A slow cold hate filled the trunk. A slow cold ocean came behind it. She drowned thinking of how much she hated Jeremiah and the deception.

Lilly came awake in her sisters arms coughing and spitting out ocean water.

She took deep breaths and rolled over on to Sher's lap and held on. She cried for what had happened to her, and to Isabella. The pain she went through, the agony. Fear was a living thing for her. Crawling up and down her spine. When she got her breath back, she sat up and looked at Isabella. They glared at each other for several minutes. Then Isabella said "Now, tell me, would you forgive him?" Her voice was quiet, but filled with rage.

Lilly was shaking with anger, fear and sadness. She wanted to hate anything and anyone right now. She wanted to lash out and hit something. She wanted to weep.

She looked at Isabella. She saw the fear, the anguish, and the unabashed hate that filled her.

"Yes, I would forgive Jeremiah. He loved you. He did not do that to you."

Isabella was taken back. She looked deeply at Lilly. All that she had just put Lilly through, and still she talks of forgiveness.

"How can you say that? Look what he did to me!"

"Isabella, he did nothing to you. He put you in a trunk for protection. He thought, with all his heart that what he was doing was going to save you, from what those men did to you."

174

She stopped for a moment. Catching her breath. Thinking of what she lived through.

"Those men who raped you deserved your anger. Those men who beat you and spit on you deserve your relentless hate. The men who threw you over board to drown, they are the ones you should have focused your merciless hate on. Not Jeremiah, not him. Him you should have forgiven years ago. He would have set you free.

They stared at each other. Minutes ticked by. Isabella's form misted and came back several times. Each time she reformed, she came back lighter. They could see the change from horrendous hatred to doubt. Then fear and understanding gripped her. She sank to her knees and wept. Lilly, Sher and Beck held onto each other. Lilly still trembling from the knowledge of Isabella's death. She hid her face in Sher's lap and cried for herself and Isabella.

The four women sat in the parlor for thirty minutes. Each in their own world, but together. The strength of each woman helping to ease the pain of the other. Isabella straightened herself, and looked at Robert.

"What do I do now Ragmar?" Her voice a mere whisper.

"You go to Jeremiah, and set him free."

"Will he take me?" She asked.

"He will take you. He has waited a long time for you. Go, forgive him."

"Will you come too?"

"Yes, I will come. I will help you cross over."

"No, Ragmar, will finally cross too?" She held out her hands for him to come with her. She could feel his pain too.

"No, I am not ready. I still have a lot to do before I can cross."

Lilly listened to them. Sher and Beck listened to. Each wondering why Robert didn't cross. And why Isabella called him Ragmar.

"Go now Isabella, before he lives through that night one more time. Free him from his guilt and shame."

Isabella looked at Lilly and her sisters.

"Thank you." She said to them. Her face was beautiful. No longer twisted in hate. Her eyes sparkled.

"I'm sorry." She was looking at Lilly. Her heart was truly in the words she spoke. Lilly had no more anger towards her. They both did what they thought was right.

Then she was gone.

And so was Robert.

# *Thirty Five*

Lilly opened the circle and released the quarters. She and Sher swept up the salt and Beck put away the candles and her book.

None of them spoke. Sher and Beck not sure what to ask Lilly. And Lilly still remembering what had happened to her. She knew it wasn't real. She knew it was dream like. But the memories were still there. Almost as if she herself had been beaten and raped.

They walked to the kitchen and sat at the table. While Sher poured them a drink. Lilly was still shaking and Beck's mind was wrapped up in her own thoughts.

Sher handed each sister a drink and leaned against the sink, finally saying "Are you alright Lil?"

Lilly turned to Sher with a smile a frail smile and shook her head yes.

"Maybe not tonight," she said. And again she fell into silence.

Several days later Robert came back. The sisters and their daughters were enjoying some time together at Beck's. While Sher and Lilly sat in lounge chairs, Beck stood at the grill, Robert appeared at the steps of the porch and spoke to them.

"She's gone. She found her peace and she left. Jeremiah with her. They both found their forgiveness."

There was a look in his eyes of distance. As if he was lost in his own thoughts of forgiveness.

"What about you?" Beck asked. Jerking him back.

"When will you find your forgiveness and cross over?" All of them waited for his answer. He looked around at them, then out to the marsh.

"It's not easy for me. There are things in my past, things I have done, I don't know if I will ever be able to cross." His eyes held a deep pain. A black hole of sorrow.

"Why? Why do you help others, but not yourself?" Lilly asked him.

"It's easier to help them. Most of them deserve to cross to the Realm of Peace. I," He couldn't finish what he was going to say. He shook his head trying to shake off the memories perhaps? They couldn't begin to guess.

When he turned to leave, Sher stopped him.

"We have a lot of questions for you." It was a simple statement. But it was endless as well.

"Yes, I know." He didn't turn to look at any of them. "Soon, I will be back soon and answer your questions. But for now relax and enjoy your selves."

They watched him walk to the edge of the marsh. He turned towards them and then was gone.

"There's a big story there, I think." Beck said to them.

"Yeah, I wonder if we want to hear it." Was Sher's answer.

"So, do we call him Robert or Ragmar?"

"Robert for now, until he tells us different." Lilly told them.

Lilly took her daughters home that night. Her house was calm. Calmer than it had been in days. Sleeping there was comfortable again. After her girls made their way upstairs to bed, she grabbed a soda and went outside. She sank into a chair and drank. She could feel herself relaxing bit by bit. And it felt good. She let her mind wander over the past few weeks, and it stopped on a thought of her mom.

"I miss you mom." She whispered. Her eyes closed, feeling the pleasure of sleep coming.

"Oh honey, I miss you too." Athena said back to her.

Lilly didn't open her eyes. She felt the warmth of her mothers voice wash over her. She smiled. A child like smile.

"I wish you were still here with me. I need you so much right now."

"You're doing fine. You are very strong Lillianna. Don't forget that."

"Do you think so? I feel so lost sometimes." Lilly felt a warm hand caress her cheek. She opened her eyes to see her mom standing over her. Athena smiled at her, and then sat in the chair next to Lilly.

"Mom?" Lilly barely spoke a word. Afraid she would break the spell she must be under.

Her mom was sitting next to her, as they had done a thousand times before she passed away. A sob caught in her throat as she said her mother's name again.

"Yes honey, I'm here." Athena reached for her daughter and pulled her into a mother's embrace. And Lilly wept. All her strength drained from her. The weeks of strain, from leaving Steve, the stress of years of staying with him. The worry and ache for her daughters, Isabella, and Robert. She let go of it all. The heart ache flowed from her. The pain and fear escaped her through her tears. In her mother's lap she cried. Athena said nothing. She didn't tell her to stop, that everything would be ok. She let her daughter cry. This was her time to let Lilly cry, to let Lilly break. When she was finished, her last tear shed, she looked up at her mom. Athena smiled her famous smile that all her daughters missed terribly.

"Am I dreaming?" She asked her mom.

"No, I'm here."

"How?"

"Thanks to Robert and you three. I don't have long though."

"Oh mom, I'm so scared."

"I know, honey. I know you are. But you're doing a great job."

"I don't feel like it, I feel like I'm failing them." Lilly looked up at the house, to where her daughters slept.

"Lilly, you need to listen to me. It isn't over. Not yet." Athena had caught her daughter's face between both of her hands. "There are a few things coming your way, you're going to have to be strong to get through them." They stared at each other for a moment.

"What mom, what's going to happen?" Fright gripped Lilly again. Cold fear edged up her spine. "Is it something with the girls?" Lilly jumped up and turned towards the house. Athena held onto her hand.

"I don't know, Lilly. I don't know what is coming for you, just know something is coming. Use your sisters. Use their strength, combine it with yours. And know that I am here. You won't always be able to see me, but know that I am always here. With all of you."

Her mind began to race. Was something going to happen to one of her girls? She didn't think she would be able to live through that. Hadn't her life been broken enough? Wasn't it her time for smooth sailing? When was it her turn to just relax? As this ran through her mind, she turned to ask her mom a question. But Athena was fading. She was not solid any more.

"Don't go mom, not yet, please don't go."

"I have to honey. I have to. Remember, I'm always here. Remember that I love you, and I'm so proud of you." Athena reached for her daughter one more time, before she could touch her, Athena was gone.

Lilly sank into the chair. She wanted to cry but the tears wouldn't come. There were none left to shed. After a few minutes, she picked up her soda and headed inside. She could feel her strength coming back to her. She welcomed it. For the first time in a long time, she felt as if she could take on anything. She felt as if she could survive what life was about to throw at her.

"Thanks mom." She said. "I can do this." She rinsed her can out, placed it in the sink and headed to bed.

"Yes, I can do this." She said again as she climbed the stairs to her room.

# Would you like to see your manuscript become a book?

If you are interested in becoming a PublishAmerica author, please submit your manuscript for possible publication to us at:

**acquisitions@publishamerica.com**

You may also mail in your manuscript to:

**PublishAmerica
PO Box 151
Frederick, MD 21705**

# www.publishamerica.com